T0129426

THE EXPATS OF SAUDI ARABIA

FERN TILDEN

BALBOA.
PRESS

A DIVISION OF HAY HOUSE

Balboa Press books may be ordered through booksellers or by contacting:

Balboa Press
A Division of Hay House
1663 Liberty Drive
Bloomington, IN 47403
www.balboapress.com
1 (877) 407-4847

Print information available on the last page.

ISBN: 978-1-5043-9645-5 (sc)
ISBN: 978-1-5043-9647-9 (hc)
ISBN: 978-1-5043-9646-2 (e)

Library of Congress Control Number: 2018901241

Balboa Press rev. date: 05/29/2018

CONTENTS

FOR EMH

Who believes this story needs to be told

February 28, 2018

"Me, go teach in Saudi Arabia? Hell no! You couldn't pay me enough to go work there. Everybody I know who went there, came back crazy."

Paige Dunhill
Canadian ESL Teacher

PREFACE

D URING MY TWO YEARS IN Saudi Arabia, I had the
opportunity to interact with expats from diverse cultures
and nations. My dear friend, EMH, who was fascinated by my
revelations, encouraged me to write this fictionalized account.
Although this book began as a story about the typical ESL teacher's
experience in Saudi Arabia based on things that I had personally
experienced or witnessed, heard about from my associates, or read
about in the newspapers, as I proceeded, I thought that it would be
more interesting and challenging to weave the tales of other expats
in the Kingdom into the basic fabric of the narrative. As such, the
characters Inga and Pamela were created, alongside a slew of minor
figures.

While this book was written for a personal reason, I believe that
it will also be of benefit to readers. By perusing this novel, I hope
that the readers will gain insight into the harsh realities of life for
numerous expats in Saudi Arabia specifically, and likewise about the
Saudi culture in general.

Similar to the pseudonymous Italian novelist, Elena Ferrante,
for better or for worse, I believe that books should stand on their
own merit. Hence, my decision to publish under a nom de plume.

Fern
Muscat, Oman

ACKNOWLEDGMENTS

THIS SPACE IS DEDICATED TO the people whom I am indebted to for making this book finally see the light of day:

Maryam Al Riyami gets my heartfelt appreciation for graciously and generously taking the time out of her busy schedule to read my draft and allowing me to bounce ideas off her. Shukran jazilan, Maryam! You rock!

Catherine Baker receives kudos for her editing prowess.

Tara Atkins, May Emerson, Rebecca Freeman, and Mary Ramirez at Balboa Press were absolute gems. Thanks to them, the publishing process went smoothly.

A final expression of gratitude goes to my beloved Uncle Al, who always supported my writing efforts and encouraged me to publish my work. Despite the spicy language sprinkled throughout this novel, I hope that I've made him proud.

CHAPTER

1

"ARE YOU A CLEANER?" THE Saudi customs officer sneers as she scans both Yasmin and her passport. Although Yasmin is fully aware that people who look like her are considered second-class citizens in the Middle East, she still bristles at the official's words. *A cleaner! How dare this semi-literate Bedu speak to me in such a condescending manner? How many bloody cleaners does she know who own a Ted Baker leather tote bag?* Yasmin calms down a tad when the thought crosses her mind that this bumpkin probably has no clue about the Ted Baker brand.

Yasmin's immediate family emigrated from the Indian subcontinent when she was two years old and settled in Britain. While her upbringing is in keeping with the Muslim traditions of the motherland, she has only visited Pakistan twice during her twenty-eight years on the planet.

Yasmin's father owns a thriving carpet business in the community of Hall Green, Birmingham. Thanks to his discipline and industry, he provides his wife and children with a solid middle-class lifestyle in London. Currently, he's grooming his one and only son to take over the business when he retires. His three daughters have all received a quality higher education. Yasmin, a graduate of the University of Bristol, with more education and cultivation under her belt than the Saudi official, isn't prepared to let the arrogant woman get away with such insolence. Counting silently to three, she composes herself. In a clipped, British accent she retorts, "No, I'm not a cleaner. It so happens that I'm a consultant for the British

1

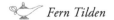

Council." The official looks at Yasmin with disdain before stamping her passport and returning it to her. Inwardly, Yasmin's seething at the slight, but refuses to give the official satisfaction in knowing the degree to which her insulting words stung. Holding her head high, she snatches her passport from the official and struts over to the conveyor belt to collect her luggage.

After collecting her suitcases, Yasmin clears customs without any further unpleasantness. In the waiting area of the terminal, she looks around for the driver that the school informed her would be picking her up. When Yasmin sees an Indian man holding a placard with her name on it, her mood improves. She puts aside the ugly incident and walks toward him.

Several minutes later, as their van weaves in and out of traffic, she looks around in excitement. The clean, wide streets are lined with sleek, imposing buildings. Some have security officers in front of them, while others are equipped with CCTVs. The massive malls, all tastefully designed, house some of the most exclusive boutiques and upscale international stores in the world. *Wow...I'm really here!* Yasmin says to herself. Silently, she thanks Allah for her good fortune in landing this job opportunity in the cosmopolitan city of Al-Khobar, Saudi Arabia.

Tired of her predictable and boring job as an adjunct professor at a community college in London, when Yasmin saw the advertisement for a start-up female college on Dave's ESL Cafe, she decided to apply. The 25 percent bonus for completing the contract is quite enticing; besides, her religion requires all able-bodied Muslims to make the Hajj Pilgrimage to Makkah once in their lifetime, and she plans to do so during this assignment.

They've got to be joking! Monica thinks to herself when she arrives at the compound at three o'clock in the morning and is told that she'll start teaching this very morning. After travelling for sixteen hours and going through several time zones, all she wants to do is sleep. She follows the affable compound manager to her apartment and deposits her luggage in a corner of the living room. Before leaving, the man cheerfully reminds Monica not to be late for the bus, which will depart promptly at 6:30 a.m.

Looking around the comfortably furnished space, Monica remarks to herself, *Not bad.* Extracting her cosmetic case from her hand luggage, she goes into the bathroom to freshen up. Her policy of always packing a night gown and some underwear in her carry-on bag pays off. Effortlessly, she finds her night gown, throws it over her head quickly, walks over to the queen-sized bed, and collapses on it. Before settling in for a nap, Monica sets her alarm clock for a quarter of six.

She's much older than the typical EFL teacher, but thanks to good genes, she is usually mistaken for a woman in her mid-thirties. While Monica loves to travel, and as a graduate student daydreamed about having a career at the United Nations, she never really had a desire to visit Saudi Arabia. The custom of segregation by gender, public executions, and whippings for offenses in this modern era, were a huge turn off to her. When the story broke about the seventy-year-old Saudi woman who had been severely flogged for talking to her stepson in public, Monica felt her pain.

However, when the United States economy took a turn for the worse in 2010 and the housing bubble burst, Monica decided to seek employment in the Middle East. Naturally, her first choice was the UAE. She had read many wonderful articles about Dubai's landmarks, shopping, and nightlife, plus the large sums of money to be made teaching EFL. If she could get her toe in the door and work in Dubai for five years, Monica had reasoned that she would be financially set for life. She had always dreamt of retiring on an exotic, Caribbean island. A nature-lover, she would be content with a property up in the hills, or by the sea. Not too big, just large enough to operate a cozy inn that would generate enough income to make her live comfortably.

As Monica read the requirements for each ad, her dream of being an inn-keeper seemed bound to remain just that – a dream. All institutions were looking to hire teachers who had previous teaching experience in the Middle East, and also a teaching license in their homeland. *So much for that idea*, Monica had sighed heavily.

Reluctantly, she turned her attention to the job opportunities in Saudi Arabia. The majority of them of course were for males, and the packages offered were very enticing. "How unfair!" Monica had muttered aloud. As she was about to exit Dave's ESL Cafe website, a message popped up: Female Teachers wanted for a Prep Year Program – Must be Able to Start Immediately! She couldn't believe the simple requirements: Must be a native speaker from the USA, Canada, or UK; possess a BA degree and a passport valid for travel for one year. Although skeptical, Monica decides to apply for the job. The following day, she was having her interview with the director. She wished that all interviews were that simple. The director had only wanted to know three things: 1) Her experiences living/traveling abroad, 2) her ability to adapt to the way of life in the conservative Saudi culture, and 3) her availability to start work as soon as her visa is approved. Satisfied with Monica's responses, the director had confirmed that she understood what she was getting herself into by accepting his offer. Although the financial benefits aren't as lucrative as other Saudi contracts advertised, Monica will still be better off working in the Kingdom than the USA. So, she had enthusiastically assured the director that she was up to the challenge. "No problem!" she had gushed. "I don't even drive back home, so the law banning women from driving doesn't affect me. I'll be sure to bring lots of books to preoccupy my free time." Confident that Monica can indeed cope with life in Saudi Arabia, the director gave her the great news that she was hired.

Loud cheers erupt on the bus as Monica and the other recently arrived teachers board. "Yay, welcome! We're so glad to see you girls!" It turns out that the other teachers had been working overtime for the past three weeks due to a staff shortage. No wonder they are so happy to see them. Monica sits beside a woman with green eyes and an alabaster complexion. From her accent, she guesses that her peer hails from one of the southern US states. They exchange pleasantries. "Hi, I'm Lauren." Monica shakes Lauren's outstretched hand and replies, "I'm Monica. Nice to meet you."

When they alight from the bus, a plump, matronly-looking woman is waiting to greet them. "Hello, welcome. I'm Susan, the head teacher. Please, come with me to my office." Susan's small office is crammed with different levels of Headway text-books and stacks of paperwork on her small desk. She gives each of the new teachers their timetable, textbooks, and office assignment. Next, she tells them the name of their coordinator and wishes them good luck. This isn't quite what Monica expects for an orientation.

Locating her office, Monica is relieved to see that she's sharing it with Lauren. Feeling at ease with Lauren, she expresses her frustration at being thrown into the classroom so soon. "I've inherited an intermediate level class and will start teaching in exactly half an hour. I'm clueless about the location of the classroom, what the students have learned so far, and where to begin in the textbook," she wails. "Don't worry," Lauren reassures her. "You'll be fine. Just ask the students what pages you should cover."

On the first day of school, Monica likes to start her class by doing introductions, icebreakers and establishing rules. She doesn't relish taking over another teacher's class and is dreading this assignment. *Fingers crossed my predecessor's style is similar to mine,* she thinks to herself as she quickly thumbs through the student book.

Lauren picks up her textbooks and throws her board markers and eraser into her bag. "Listen, I've gotta go," she tells Monica as she heads out the door. "A few words of advice:

1. The students run the show here, keep them happy if you want to keep your job.
2. Wasta, or Vitamin W, is the supplement of choice here. Students will use it to get their poor attendance and failing grades changed, and even to switch classes.

3. Don't discuss politics, sex, or religion with your students.
4. Don't force the Sunni and Shia students to work together.

If you keep these things in mind, you'll be fine." As Lauren turns the door handle she cautions, "Oh! One more thing, watch your back."

CHAPTER

2

IF A FORTUNE-TELLER WOULD HAVE told me five years ago, "Inga, you're going to marry an exotic man from a distant land and bear him two adorable kids," I would have told her that she was full of prunes and demanded my money back. However, that's exactly what happened! Being a career-oriented woman, quite frankly, I had no desire to marry or start a family; but life does indeed have a way of happening when we're busy making other plans. After completing my MBA in investment banking, I decided to take a gap year to backpack around the globe. So, in the summer of 2010, I bought me an around-the-world-ticket and set off on the first leg of my journey from Stockholm to the UAE.

As luck would have it, when I arrived at the check-in counter at London Heathrow airport, the agent informed me that the flight was thirteen passengers overbooked and inquired if I would be willing to take the next flight later that day. Since I had no fixed itinerary for my trip to Dubai, and was in no hurry, I offered to give up my seat. As compensation for volunteering to be bumped, I was upgraded to the First-Class cabin. Lady Luck was still smiling on me, as I was assigned a seat next to a handsome young man with intense dark brown eyes and a sexy beard. We struck up a harmless conversation about the hassles and rewards of traveling and agreed that despite the aggravation, travel is still a worthwhile endeavor. Throughout the flight, we got to know each other better. He informed me that his name was Khalid and he was a graduate student at the London School of Economics. I almost fell off my seat when he revealed that he was from Saudi Arabia. He totally did not fit the stereotype of the typical Saudi man, one who is pompous and painfully provincial. Curious about life in his homeland, I peppered him with questions: "Is it true that a quarter of Saudi Arabians live in poverty?" "What do you think about Sharia law?" "How do you feel about Saudi women demanding the right to drive in the kingdom?" While it was evident that he didn't particularly relish my line of inquiry, he was most gracious and - I thought - honest in his reply.

Since I had thoroughly enjoyed Khalid's company during the flight, and feelings were clearly mutual, when we landed in Dubai, I eagerly exchanged email addresses with him. I cannot tell a lie, I was looking forward to keeping in touch with him and secretly hoped that he and I would see each other again. The universe has a way of conspiring to make our wishes come true. So, it should come as no surprise, that Khalid and I became email pals for the remainder of my whirl around the world. While I was enjoying my solo adventures, a part of me began to wish that Khalid could be by my side to share these new experiences with me. I know this must sound crazy to some of you, but it's true. I guess that's how I knew I was falling in love with him.

The end of my travels corresponded with the end of Khalid's studies. He completed his degree in Economics and graduated with honors. To celebrate his achievement and my "homecoming" we spent a glorious weekend in the Paddington district prior to his family's arrival. We had fun strolling through Hyde Park and Kensington Gardens, eating fish and chips at the Summerhouse and even managed to squeeze in a romantic boat ride along the Regent's Canal to the picturesque district of Little Venice. Our last night together in London, Khalid proposed, and I readily accepted. You can well imagine how hard it was for me to say good-bye to him and board the flight to Sweden the following morning.

Naturally, arriving at my parents' home in Stockholm, was bittersweet. I was happy to be home and see them; but sad that shortly I would be leaving them again. This time for good. It took me a while to muster the courage to tell them that I was engaged. That news would have shocked them enough since I had not previously mentioned to them that I was dating anybody. However, the additional knowledge that I was going to marry a Saudi would have broken their hearts. So, I postponed having this conversation with them.

In the interim, I regaled them with stories about my travels on each continent. Sail fishing on the Pacific Coast of Guatemala was exhilarating. Catching a 25kg fish and spending 30 minutes trying to reel it in gave me one of the biggest adrenalin rushes in my life. Salsa dancing the night away to infectious beats at shabby cafes in Havana with the locals was a dream come true. Trekking for four days in Nepal's unadulterated Himalayas took me out of my comfort zone and deepened my spirituality. Roaming the medieval pathways of the medina in Fez, admiring the ceramic mosaics on buildings, and haggling with the souq sellers over traditional lanterns and ornamental tagines was absolute fun. Visiting the Asmat tribe in Papua New Guinea and observing their daily rituals was quite fascinating. And so on...

Sharing these cultural tidbits about the highlights of my travel adventures with my parents ended up being a good move on my part. After circumnavigating them around the world through my stories and photos, they discussed taking a trip to Asia. Although my mother and father had travelled extensively throughout Europe, they had never left the continent. So, I was pleasantly surprised when they told me that I had inspired them to visit Bali on their next vacation. Their revelation eased my guilty conscience somewhat about keeping Khalid and our engagement a secret.

Three weeks later, a recruiter notified me that a well-known women's university in Riyadh was actively seeking business instructors. So, without any qualms, I promptly applied for the position. To be honest with you, I never had a desire to become a teacher; my goal had always been to work at a prestigious financial institution in Stockholm. However, now that I was engaged and

quite keen on being reunited with my beloved, I jumped at the opportunity. The interview went well, and I was offered the job. Therefore, I took it.

I'm ashamed to tell you that despite having a wonderful relationship with my parents, and although I was about to leave them shortly, I still could not bring myself to tell them that I was engaged. Yes, that was quite cowardly of me, but I knew that my mother and father wouldn't approve of my decision or understand. So, when my employment paperwork had been processed and I had received my multiple entry visa, I simply told them that I had received a job offer in Riyadh and was going to live and work there for a couple of years. Naturally, hearing all the horror stories about how women are treated in Saudi Arabia, they were not thrilled with my news and begged me to reconsider my plan. "Wouldn't it be better for you to work in Dubai instead, dear?" my father pleaded, to which my mother nodded her head in support. However, when I stood firm, in the end, they grudgingly accepted my decision and half-heartedly gave me their blessings.

CHAPTER

3

RUEFULLY, PAMELA ADMIRES THE EXQUISITE ruby and sapphire bracelet intricately set in 22-karat Saudi gold. It is her latest acquisition from her husband, Glenn. She must admit, he has excellent taste in jewelry. In happier times, such lavish gifts had been sufficient to placate her after they had a spat over her desire to return to Texas, settle down and start their family. Glenn would always end up telling Pamela that the time wasn't right, and she would inevitably burst into tears. Then, he would relent and buy her a stunning piece of jewelry that made her the envy of her girlfriends. Their last argument netted her a Tiffany gold locket, while their previous squabble had gained her a Cartier Love Ring. Today, such consolation gifts no longer cut it with Pamela. She was done shedding tears and waiting for the right time.

Gently, Pamela put the precious bracelet back in its box. Firmly, she closed the lid and placed the box back on her vanity set. She looked at Glenn, snug under their pure, Egyptian cotton sateen bed sheets. She studied his handsome face for a minute and listened to his gentle snores. Slowly, she eased herself on the bed, so as not to wake him. Kissing him lightly on the cheek, she whispered, "Baby, you've changed."

Pamela and Glenn met at McGill University seventeen years ago. Both of them were ambitious, international students enrolled at the prestigious College of Engineering. She grew up in a conservative, middle class family in San Antonio, Texas, while Glenn hailed from the laid-back, liberal Caribbean island of Barbados. Despite their differences in upbringing, they connected over science and their love of travel. By sophomore year, they were inseparable. They spent many hours studying together, dreaming about traveling the world, listening to reggae music, and cooking Caribbean food in their little apartment. During their junior year, Pamela and Glenn talked about having a future life together with two kids. They introduced each other to their respective families and got engaged. The day after they graduated magna cum laude from McGill University, they were wed in a civil wedding ceremony in San Antonio.

Both Pamela and Glenn thought that it would be exciting to work in the Middle East for several years. So, when one of the leading oil companies in Saudi Arabia recruited Glenn for a position paying six figures, they jumped at the opportunity. They had an understanding - or at least Pamela thought that they did - they were going to stay in Dhahran for four years. That would give them sufficient time to repay their student loans and travel to the UAE and Africa. At the end of four years, they were going to return to Texas and buy a condo in the Riverwalk section of San Antonio.

Those four years came and went quickly. As planned, they had repaid their college loans in full and had even managed to vacation in the UAE and Jordan. Another four years passed them by in the Kingdom. They had done very well with their savings and visited the African continent twice. The first time, they traveled to Morocco and Tunisia. On their second trip, they went on safari in Tanzania, and likewise, vacationed in Zanzibar. "We've done good, babe," Pamela recalled saying to Glenn at the end of their eighth year. "It's time for us to return home." Her pleas were invariably met with Glenn's justifications for why the timing wasn't ideal for him to resign from the oil company. There was always a project that needed to be finished, or one about to start that required his expertise. And so, it continued.

Glenn and Pamela were now mid-way through their eleventh year. In a couple of months, she'd be turning thirty-five. She had expected to have given birth to their children by now, be settled back

12

home in the comfortable routine of parenting and working part-time in her field. The last time she had gently broached the subject with Glenn about returning West and starting a family, he had exploded. "Dammit, Pam! Do you know how many women would love to be in your Jimmy Choos? Living the Life of Riley as we do in this beautiful villa maintained by a house-keeper? Holidaying in exotic places and shopping at the most exclusive boutiques on the planet? We've got a good thing going, sugar. Why do you want to muck up our lives with kids?"

Glenn's outburst had shocked Pamela. He had never previously raised his voice at her, or spoken so plainly about no longer wanting to have children. Was this really him speaking, or was this the stress from his job talking? Pamela knew that Glenn was under a lot of pressure at work. He had a very demanding position, and the additional stress of having to prove himself competent in an environment that didn't value or think highly of black men. It didn't matter that he had graduated with honors from an elite university. In the Middle East, he was judged inferior, solely because of the color of his skin. Despite the unhealthy work milieu and the fact that they were financially secure, Glenn seemed unwilling to walk away and leave it all behind. From his last comment, Pamela had to admit to herself that her husband had no intention of leaving his lucrative career anytime soon. And worse, he didn't plan to make good on his promise of having children with her.

As Pamela mulled over these truths, she became very resentful of Glenn. She had believed him when he had told her that they would do a stint in Saudi Arabia then return home to start a family. She had sacrificed a lot both personally and professionally when she came with him to this wretched country. Over the years, the distance had taken a toll on her friendships back home. On the occasions that she returned to Texas for a visit, she could tell that her relationships with friends had changed. There would be nothing to talk about during their reunions because she didn't want to sound as if she was bragging about her glamorous life of ease. And of course, very little had occurred in the time that she'd left home that was newsworthy of her friends to share. After a while, folks would look at her differently and make excuses for not being able to get together when she was in town. Pamela understood clearly that this was due to their inability to identify with her perceived fabulous lifestyle.

Then there was the huge loss of independence that Pamela also had to forfeit when she followed Glenn to Saudi Arabia. It was bad enough that her ability to drive a vehicle was suspended while living in the Kingdom, but the added insult of needing to obtain Glenn's permission if she wanted to go to the doctor/hospital, leave the country, or travel somewhere without him, was really beginning to tick her off.

Thinking about her career being placed on pause indefinitely while Glenn advanced in his, also rankled Pamela. Due to gender discrimination in the Kingdom, she has no chance of working at an oil company. The role of engineer is strictly reserved for men. So, her days are spent on their beautiful compound socializing with the wives of other expat executives and engineers.

She would be a liar, if she claimed not to enjoy the charmed, over-indulgent compound lifestyle she had grown accustomed to over the past ten years. Which woman in her right mind wouldn't delight in being pampered with weekly trips to the nail and hair salons? Or rejoice in not having to do domestic chores? Pamela would be a hypocrite if she denied her good fortune in marrying a man who would be considered a "great catch" by women with high standards. Glenn, was very attentive, a wonderful provider, and companion. Except for enjoying a quality Cuban cigar now and again, he was free from truly harmful vices like mistresses, alcohol, and gambling. Yes, she had indeed hit the jackpot and had nothing to complain about. Apart from this issue of Glenn no longer desiring children, he had measured up as a husband. Of course, Pamela also understood quite well that no relationship is ever split 50-50. One partner always gives more than the other. She was painfully aware of this truth and the fact that many women would gladly trade places with her. Some people might even think that Pamela was a complete fool to entertain thoughts of repudiating her refined and gracious lifestyle for the sake of procreating. Right or wrong, with all that she had sacrificed, Pamela was beginning to feel that she was getting the short end of the stick in her marriage.

15

CHAPTER
4

YASMIN WIPES HER SWEATY BROW with her arm. *They weren't kidding when they said that this is a start-up,* she grumbles before guzzling half of the water in her plastic bottle. The interior of the newly built college was a shambles. Blue plastic bags, empty water bottles, and remnants of the construction workers' lunches were strewn across the floors. It looked like the space had been ravaged by a tornado. After Yasmin catches her breath, she resumes picking up the trash until it's time for her lunch break. All teachers had been assigned a certain area of the college to clean up. She's impressed that nobody was whinging about this dirty job that wasn't in their job description. Admirably, all admins, teachers and learning coaches were working together to get the school ready for the grand opening in ten days' time.

Her next task is to clean the latrines on the second floor in Block A. Ever since getting stuck in a lift for several hours as a child, Yasmin has always preferred to take the stairs. So, she drags her tired self, up the two flights of stairs. The overpowering stench from the WCs hits her nose sharply when she reaches the landing on the second floor. They reek of rancid human waste. Feeling the bile rising to the back of her throat, she quickly puts her hand to her mouth and leans against the wall. "You alright?" asked a concerned voice. Yasmin turned around and saw the head English teacher, Vicki. Although she felt squeamish, she put on a brave face and nodded her head. Convinced that Yasmin was fine, Vicki soon disappeared back down the hallway.

The smell inside the latrine is unbearable. Yasmin holds her breath, quickly dons her thick, yellow latex gloves and hastily squirts toilet bowl cleaner in each toilet. She then dashes out of the WCs and exhales. Twenty minutes later, she reluctantly returns to complete her task. *They're so lucky that I'm a team player!* Yasmin thought to herself as she took a deep breath and gave each toilet bowl a good scrub down. Next, she cleaned the mirrors above the face basins and mopped the floor. Finally, she sprayed an entire can of Lysol disinfectant throughout the WCs.

When Yasmin discarded her rubber gloves at the end of the workday, she was completely knackered, but also chuffed at the great job she'd done in the restroom. Every stall and washbasin was spotless, and the air smelt fresh. Yasmin had heard that Saudis are by nature litterbugs; judging by the trash littering the streets, she believed this to be the case. She cringed at the thought that when the college opens, the WCs will revert to their former grossness. *I sincerely hope that the dean plans to hire custodial staff to clean the latrines and other spaces,* Yasmin thought to herself. *If she doesn't, I'm going to be a very unhappy camper if this becomes my regular duty.*

Getting the college rooms in shape for students and staff was just the first step. The bigger challenge however, was the recruiting of students, sourcing of classroom furniture, school supplies, and text books. Despite the dean's reassurances that desks, chairs, computers and projectors were on the way and "Inshallah" would arrive by the end of the week, Yasmin wasn't as optimistic. If she had been in charge, she would have done things in reverse. First, she would have conducted research to assess the community's interest in a vocational college. Depending on the survey results, she would know how to proceed with the ordering of the school furniture and equipment, plus different levels of English textbooks. Until these shipments were safely in country, Yasmin would have deferred making a public announcement of the college's Grand Opening. *Oh well, I'm not being paid the big bucks to do all this thinking,* she

muttered to herself. *I'll bet my first paycheck though, we'll be at sixes and sevens for a long time.*

Monica massaged her temples and sighed loudly as she wondered what she had gotten herself into. *This place is a trip and a half! It's a good thing that Saudi Arabia is a dry kingdom,* she thought to herself. Although Monica is not a drinker, with all that she's dealt with during her first two weeks, she could easily develop a close friendship with Bombay Sapphire London Dry Gin and Schweppes Tonic Water. Up until now, she had never worked in a place so disorganized, or in a culture that was so strange. One really needed a lot of patience and a great sense of humor to survive Saudi Arabia with his/her sanity intact.

Having to deal with all these restrictions on freedom, Monica felt like she was always walking on eggshells. For starters, she had to be very careful about not offending her students and had to run all classroom ideas by her coordinator to ensure that they were appropriate. Naturally, games such as hangman - which are perfect to practice spelling - and the use of music and songs to review lessons is haram (forbidden). If Monica wanted to show her students a movie so they could later do a writing assignment or speaking activity, she must first get permission from her supervisor. And so, she found all these procedures stressful and her creativity waning.

Being herself a product of co-ed institutional learning and having previously taught English in Japan to co-ed university students, coming to Saudi Arabia and teaching female-only university students who primarily came to school to socialize was a big shock for Monica. Sometimes, while writing the aim of the lesson on the white board, she would turn around and see some students lacquering their fingernails, others busy styling their friends' tresses, while the very bold ones sat cross-legged on a mat in the back of the room chitchatting in Arabic, drinking coffee and munching dates.

Monica had never seen anything like this before. Very few students came to class prepared to learn English. Even fewer came with their homework assignments completed. It drove Monica nuts when her students would tell her that they forgot to do their homework, or forgot to bring their text books and writing implements.

Often, she wished that they would just "forget" to come to class. Of course, there was no chance of that happening because the Saudi king gives his subjects an attractive stipend to attend college. If it weren't for this financial incentive, Monica was absolutely sure that her classes would be empty. It took her a while to get used to this fact, but now that she understood the system, she was learning to go with the flow.

Putting herself in her students' designer shoes, Monica could, however, empathize with their desire to socialize during class time to a certain extent. After all, this was the only time they had to interact with people who weren't related to them. Their lunch break was only half an hour long and during that time, they must also make time to pray. Furthermore, their male relatives drove them to school in the mornings, and immediately after classes ended, whisked them home. In this culture, females are conditioned to stay at home. So, at the end of the school day, they stay indoors with their mother and sisters unless the family decides to take a trip to the mall, or a relative's house. This was also the norm for them on weekends too.

As you probably already know, Saudis tend to marry young. So, although Monica's students ranged in age from seventeen to nineteen years old, many of them were already married with children. She found it difficult to picture them as parents because they were just kids themselves and most of them tended to be immature. However, in all fairness to them, they were not given the chance to grow up and take responsibility for themselves. Their fathers/uncles/brothers run their lives for them until they get married, and then their husbands/ sons are given the reins of control. As such, a Saudi female cannot attend university, travel, work, or receive major medical treatment without her guardian's consent. On a positive, Monica thought that it must be nice for females never to have to worry about housing, the payment of bills, or employment. Those issues are strictly the concerns of the Saudi males.

Monica had noticed that a good number of the students at the university where she's employed clearly have a learning disability. She wondered if this was also the case at other institutions across the Kingdom, and thought that it would be interesting to see scientific research conducted, to assess the roots of this phenomenon. Monica wouldn't be surprised however, if this trend was a result of the Saudis' custom of marrying their first cousins.

Regarding her work week, at first, it felt weird to her not going to work on Fridays and going to work on Sundays. However, Monica eventually got used to the system. Whether she was off on Friday and Saturday, or Saturday and Sunday, the bottom line was that she still got two days off, and that was the important thing. The expats in the Kingdom who are manual laborers only got one day to rest every week.

Although she had only arrived a fortnight ago, for all intents and purposes, Monica was pretty much settled into her apartment. Since she only planned to stay for one year, she was not going to get carried away with making the place too homey. She did, however, buy a small, colorful, wool rug for her bedroom. To break up the drabness of concrete, she also purchased two medium-sized desert scene paintings to hang on the living room walls, and a large philodendron plant to beautify the balcony.

This evening, Monica is going to a staff social function. She has two hours to kill before meeting Lauren. Together, they're going to attend the poolside party that's being held at their compound. Monica is a bit apprehensive about going to the party because of Saudi Arabia's strict laws governing the social interaction of unrelated men and women. She had heard that two years earlier, several Arab expats in Riyadh who had organized a co-ed party at which alcohol was served, received prison terms and 100 lashes each. Anyhow, she went along to the party because she figured that if there was a police raid, the director who had organized the event would be the one to take the fall – not her. At seven sharp, Monica met Lauren in front of her apartment. Lauren was wearing a cute, floral summer dress and strappy sandals. This led Monica to second guess her choice of outfit: a white cotton T-shirt and navy-blue pedal pushers. As they walked over to the pool, Monica inquired amiably, "So, how did you make out at the mall?"

"Great, thanks for asking. I bought some cushions for the sofa, a blender, and a food processor," Lauren replied with a wide smile. "When we get paid," she continued, "I'm going to buy some bed and bath linens too." Monica's face lit up at the prospect of receiving her very first paycheck in two weeks' time. "Ooh, I can't wait for payday!" she exclaimed. "To celebrate, I might even accompany you to the mall, Lauren."

As they approached the area where the party was being held, they could hear hip-hop music lightly playing. This was quite risky, since music is forbidden in the Kingdom. Some of their colleagues frolicked in the pool, while others lounged around it in clusters – smoking, gossiping and swaying their bodies to the music. Many of the women looked very different with their hair curled, and faces made up. They strutted around in their high heels and flirted with the guys. A couple of the men were grilling BBQ burgers, chicken, and camel meat. Nearby, two square, plastic tables had been joined together and were laden with bottles of water, cans of fruit juices, and soda. Monica grabbed a cup of mango nectar for herself and a lime mint for Lauren. While they sipped their beverages, they surveyed the scene. Monica was about to ask Lauren if she would like a refill when Lauren nudged her. She followed Lauren's gaze with her eyes. Two of the men had just brought out some bottles of moonshine. Monica raised her eyebrow and whispered to Lauren, "Are these jokers for real? This is not the country to be playing the fools."

Shortly afterwards, Lauren gasped and pointed at the pool. Monica looked and blinked twice just before they both heard a loud splash. They looked at each other in disbelief. Did they just see their supervisor, Libby, stripped down to her birthday suit, jump into the pool with Larry and Donald? "Oh No She Didn't! Lauren, please tell me that our eyes are playing tricks on us," said Monica. Still shaking her head in amazement, Lauren replied, "Honey, I wish I could, but Libby sure did just go skinny-dipping!" Lauren took a delicate sip of her drink, then added with an impish grin, "Ooh, Donald better hope that this news doesn't reach his wife's ears back in Manitoba." Monica looked at her and whispered, "Say whaaat? He's married? I didn't notice him wearing a wedding band." Lauren rolled her eyes as she swirled the ice in her cup. "Oh yeah, he's very much married. Just like most of his ringless buddies you see hooking up with these ladies." Monica glanced around the pool and noticed a lot of couples canoodling. "Wow, these people don't waste time, do they?" she replied. This wasn't her idea of a party. So, after gulping down the remainder of her juice, she stood up and said, "Lauren, this isn't my scene, I'm gonna bounce!" "Me too," Lauren replied. Together, they hastily slipped away through the shrubs into the falling darkness.

CHAPTER

5

I ALMOST DIDN'T RECOGNIZE KHALID WHEN we saw each other a few days after my arrival in Riyadh. He looked so different wearing a thobe, ghoutrah and agal. "You look so GQ with that tablecloth on your head," I teased him. He has a great sense of humor, and laughed heartily. Since Saudi law forbids social interaction between males and females who aren't related, Khalid and I were forced to resort to clandestine rendezvous. Usually, we would meet at the corniche when the sun was setting. Other times, I would slip into the back seat of his Jaguar Range Rover and lay down low, as he drove us to a remote spot in the desert. When the coast was clear, he would open the back door and I would emerge with my niqab covering my face. Sometimes, we would have a picnic, but most times, we would just talk and watch the sun set. Oh, how I valued those precious hours that we could be together.

For romantic weekends, we had to travel to Bahrain or Oman because couples cannot check into hotels in Saudi Arabia without presenting a valid marriage certificate. Apart from the opportunity for intimacy, I loved these little getaways because they offered us the freedom to express ourselves openly. It was awesome dining together, going to the cinema, or simply holding hands while we walked around the city.

Like me, Khalid had not told his family about us yet. He felt that it was too soon to break the news. Having been gone for seven years, he wanted to become reacquainted with his family first, before dropping this bomb on them. Since he was almost 27, he knew that

23

it was only a matter of time before his mother would broach the subject of choosing a wife. Then, he planned to tell her about me. At first, I was a little worried that his mother would disapprove of me, but Khalid allayed my fears by telling me that his mother had no problem with him dating Western women while he lived in London. "Dating and marrying are two different things," I reminded him. But he reassured me that we would cross that bridge when we got to it.

In preparation for my new life as a Saudi wife, I thought it would be a great idea to take Arabic lessons. This gesture would certainly put me in good graces with Khalid's family. My employer offered Arabic courses at a discount rate; so, three nights a week, I studied beginner's level Arabic with several colleagues. It was quite challenging for me to learn Arabic, which made me sympathetic to my students who struggled with their English language skills. Thank God, I really don't need to master Arabic because Khalid's relatives are all fluent in English. Anyhow, I still did my best to learn a few basic expressions that would come in handy when I went shopping or needed to take a taxi. Besides, I thought that Khalid would be pleased that I was making the effort to assimilate in his culture.

Although I'm not overly fond of Saudi cuisine, I believed it would be beneficial to learn how to prepare a few popular Saudi dishes properly. After all, it's been said that the way to a man's heart is through his belly. So, my being able to cook Arabic food well would make Khalid happy. Another benefit was the favorable light in which I would be viewed by my soon-to-be in-laws. So, several nights a week, I tried to make some recipes - that I found online - for halwa, kabsa, and biriyani. When I was satisfied with my kitchen prowess, one evening I surprised Khalid with a few home cooked dishes to see if they met with his approval. I'm pleased to report that they did and there was no food leftover.

I had noticed that whenever he and I dined out, Khalid always ate western food – the triumvirate of pasta, pizza, and potatoes to be exact. I'm not sure if that's because he was with me, or because he had lived in London, or because he simply wanted a change from the typical Arab diet that he ate at home. Regardless, that suited me just fine, because I'm a pro at making lasagna, and hearty stews with potatoes. Besides, having the option to rotate our meals between Arabic and Western style dishes, would make my life easier and palate happier.

The one western food product that I was sorely going to miss eating when I married Khalid was pork. Bacon, ham, pork chops, spare ribs, and sausage were some of my favorite foods. Every now again, I liked to enjoy a pork dish with a glass of white or red wine. Although pig products are banned in Saudi Arabia, wouldn't you know it, there are certain shops on the black market in Bahrain that sell bacon and ham to Muslims. Of course, it's risky trying to smuggle this contraband into Saudi Arabia, but I've noticed that the border officials don't really search us expats. Their primary concern is with their compatriots who sometimes get busted for possessing liquor, or you guessed it – pork. I suppose that's because in their religion, consuming alcohol and eating pig byproducts is against the teachings of the Qur'an.

One of the most difficult questions that I've ever been asked pertained to the consumption of pork. The question itself was not complex. In fact, it was quite simple. So simple that even a five-year-old would be able to answer it. So, when my beloved one night stared at me out of his big, intelligent eyes and shyly asked, "Inga, how does pork taste?" I had difficulty articulating an intelligent answer to his question. Perhaps, it would be more accurate to say that I was stumped. Yes, me, Ms. Lover-of-Words, was now at a loss for words. Honestly, prior to Khalid's inquiry, I had never given much thought to how pork tasted. I was raised on it and always thought it delicious whether baked, barbequed, or fried. Somehow, a response of, "Well, it tastes like pig," seemed crass. And so, for a second, I entertained the thought of this very simple and effective, solution... offering Khalid a forkful of my bacon and eggs and letting him decide for himself. However, that too would have been inappropriate. So, for what it was worth, I ended up saying, "It tastes okay, but lamb and chicken are by far tastier."

 *Fern Tilden*

For the record, Khalid did not force me to convert to his faith. I did so of my own free will. This might sound shallow, but the truth of the matter is that my decision to convert to Islam was to a large extent influenced by my desire to make my upcoming marriage work. I just felt that it would be better for all parties involved, if we were on the same page culturally. Now, don't get me wrong, my decision to convert doesn't mean that I totally agreed with all the teachings of the Qur'an. As a matter of fact, I took issue - and still do - with the Muslim man having the right to marry four wives, while Muslim women can only have one husband; ditto the law that grants Saudi husbands the right to divorce their wives on a whim, while Saudi wives must go through a painful and arduous process if they choose to initiate the divorce. Regardless, I still think that I made the right decision to marry Khalid and convert to Islam.

CHAPTER

6

PAMELA STIFLED A YAWN AS her lunch mate, Angel, droned on and on about her recent trip to Oman. She kept on rehashing her experience in Muscat and how the local men were hitting on her. "So, I had just taken a dip in the water at Fins Beach and was getting ready to work on my tan, when this young stud muffin sauntered over to me…" *Gosh, is this what my life has been reduced to now – meaningless drivel?* Pamela wondered to herself. Ironically, in the not-so-distant past, Pamela had thrived on this very "drivel" and looked forward to her weekly lunch dates with Angel and the other expat wives.

When her companion paused to look at the dessert menu, Pamela discreetly looked around the Madeleine French Bakery & Brasserie. This was one of her favorite eateries in Al Khobar. She just loved the quirky décor, the atmosphere and desserts. A young European mother, who was sitting a few tables away, caught her eye. They exchanged a brief smile before the mother returned her attention to her infant. Softly, she cooed to her baby in the stroller. Pamela wished that she could hold the child, but resisted the urge to walk over to the mother and request her permission.

"…and then he said, 'Maash'allah! Would you like some help putting on your lotion?'" And I said, "I'm managing just fine, thank you very much!" Then he said, "Can I buy you a Red Bull?" and I said, "My body is my temple, I don't fill it with junk." And then he whispered, "I'd really like to come over and worship at your temple." And I said, "Oh, I bet you would. What's in it for me? And …"

Snapping out of her trance like state, Pamela directed her attention to Angel. "That's a good one," she stated absentmindedly - not entirely sure what her buddy had said. She was relieved when she spotted the waiter making a beeline for their table. With a flourish, he placed their food in front of them. Angel immediately focused her energy on eating her bread pudding.

Since Angel was preoccupied with her dessert, Pamela stole another glance at the young woman and her baby. She admired her for raising a child in this environment. Weather aside, there was no way that Pamela would be rearing her kids in Saudi Arabia. The segregation along gender lines and restrictions in personal liberties could do a lot of psychological damage to her offspring – or anybody else's for that matter. Adult expats here have a hard-enough time coping with this culture; it would be unconscionable to impose such a lifestyle on children. Besides, it was important to Pamela that her children be well-rounded and exposed to people from different cultures and walks of life. If she had a son, he must grow up with Glenn's respect and appreciation for females. In the event she was blessed with a daughter, she wanted her to inherit her spirit of independence, have the right to be her own person, and make her own choices in life.

"Angel," Pamela began hesitantly. "A friend of mine back home recently asked my advice on a personal matter and I wanted to get your thoughts on the issue before I got back to her." Angel smiled broadly, clearly pleased that Pamela valued her input. She put her fork down and said, "Shoot."

"Now, this is just between you and me," Pamela clarified before proceeding.

"Mum's the word," Angel promised.

"Well, when my friend and her hubby first decided to get married, they had talked about starting a family once they got their finances and careers in order. A decade later, they're quite prosperous, but her hubby has changed his mind about having kids."

"Bastard," Angel hissed and scowled.

"My friend is devastated because she really loves her hubs, but she also wants to have children."

"I see," replied Angel. She played with the crumbs on her plate with her fork for a while before adding, "In that case, since the man no longer wants to have kids, and it's not a matter of him being impotent, but your friend desperately wants to have her own children - but isn't open to adoption, I'd advise her to pack her bags and leave. The longer she stays in her marriage, the more she'll regret not having had any children. Then this regret is going to grow into resentment of her spouse and their lives are going to be hell together. So, it's best that she cuts her losses now and moves on before it's too late. If her hubby really loves her, he'll understand her decision. And maybe later, they can reconcile and even remain friends."

"Thanks, Angel...those were my sentiments exactly."

Later that evening, Pamela felt a pang of guilt when Glenn arrived home. As she greeted him with her customary hug and peck on the lips, her mind flashed to the story of Judas who is about to betray Jesus. "Dear, I was thinking," she said to Glenn, "Since you're going to be away on business all of next month, I'll go back to Texas and visit my folks." Glenn made himself comfortable in his favorite recliner and replied, "Sure, honey. That's a great idea. Ayu's due her vacation time, so I'll approve for her to go back to Jakarta during the period we're away." Pamela flashed her husband a wide smile and said, "Perfect. I'll go ahead and book my flight." As she walked towards their study, Glenn blurted out, "When we get back, we'll celebrate your birthday, sugar." Pamela was close to tears. Times like this, she wished that Glenn wasn't such a terrific husband. If he were lousy, that would have made her decision to leave so much easier. Her mind replayed all the thoughtful things he had done for her, all the great times and conversations they had shared. He is one of the few men she knows who still opens doors and pulls out chairs for ladies,

29

and buys flowers even when it's not Valentine's Day, or her birthday. It's truly unfortunate that he no longer wanted to have children. Pamela is positive that Glenn would make an awesome dad. *Maybe, he'll change his mind after I'm gone*, she thought hopefully.

Part of her felt that she owed it to Glenn to tell him upfront that she was leaving him, but the rational side of her knew this wouldn't be prudent. She could see herself being convinced by him to rethink the matter. Well, Pamela was done with re-thinking, she knew that Angel was right. The longer she hung in there, the more miserable and resentful she would become of Glenn. Besides, it wouldn't be fair to spring this decision on him right now – especially since he's preoccupied with a project at work. No, it's better to keep him in the dark until she's back in Texas.

CHAPTER

7

THIS MAY SOUND PITIFUL, BUT the sad truth is that Yasmin's weekly shopping trips to the mall and hypermarket are the highlight of her life in Al-Khobar. How embarrassing! She can't even bring herself to admit this pathetic truth to her family back home in Birmingham. Anyhow, it's currently the story of her life. You've got to remember that women here have many restrictions imposed on their mobility. They can't drive and are forbidden to go into the desert; some restaurants are off-limits to females, and there are no discotheques, movie theaters, bars, night clubs, or bowling alleys. Their only options for recreation are to sit in a park or go shopping. The park and corniche nearby Yasmin's compound are very nice. However, they are usually crowded with Saudi families. Since she kind of sticks out like a sore thumb and can't stand being gawked at, she seldom goes to these places.

The malls are very large and posh. The two most popular ones are Rashid Mall and the Mall of Dhahran. They're so huge, it would take an entire day to walk from one end to the other. Naturally, they're always packed with Saudi women and children. When Yasmin is in the mood for international food, she goes to these malls and treats herself to Costa coffee and Cinnabon pastries. Since she's trying to be healthy, she refrains from eating fast food on a regular basis. Now and again, she has a craving for KFC or McDonald's and will yield to temptation.

Since the merchandise in the stores at these malls is very expensive, Yasmin rarely buys anything there. Although she can financially afford to treat herself to a few luxury items every couple of months, she just can't bring herself to spend that kind of money. She was raised in a household where materialism is frowned upon and frugality is valued. Therefore, when she goes to the malls, she usually just sits with her snack and indulges in a bit of people-watching. It's harmless fun for Yasmin to observe the Saudi women go by with their shopping bags from stores such as Cerruti, DKNY, Lacoste, and Swarovski. She enjoys trying to guess the contents of their bags.

Funny but true, Yasmin's favorite kind of shopping here is grocery shopping. That's right, grocery shopping. While the average person might think that Yasmin's life sounds very dry, she really looks forward to the weekly compound bus trips to Tamimi Markets. The extent to which Yasmin enjoys these outings is apparent by her constantly singing Sheikh Tamimi's praise for this simple pleasure. Due to his vision, the Kingdom's first modern supermarket was opened in Al-Khobar in 1979. Appropriately named in his honor, this chain of supermarkets offers a wide selection of local, regional, and international foods and household products.

On her first trip to Tamimi's, Yasmin became a little emotional when she saw all her beloved UK brands there: Alpen Muesli, McVities biscuits, Walkers Shortbread. If she'd known that they were so readily available in the Kingdom, she wouldn't have laden her luggage with boxes of these items. Yasmin had fun pushing her trolley down the long, clean aisles filled with name brand food and household products from different regions of the world. While this simple pleasure might not be viewed as a big deal by the average expat going grocery shopping, this was special to Yasmin. Having visited acquaintances in the dusty town of Al Ahsa in the Eastern province, she knew that she had got a good thing going in Al Khobar. Things could be a whole lot worse if she were living in other less developed regions of Saudi Arabia. Occasionally, she even encountered expats living in Al Ahsa shopping at Tamimi's. Their presence at Tamimi's proved that they lacked quality shopping venues in their neighborhoods. Anyhow, from Yasmin's personal experience, she knew that there's nothing "super" about supermarkets in the smaller towns and villages. They're more like mini-marts. They have narrow aisles and an even narrower selection of imported goods. Expats can forget about buying Earl Grey Tea, and organic foodstuff like kale and chia seeds in those places. If they are lucky enough to find a box of Carr's water crackers or Dorset cereal, they should give themselves a pat on the back. And stock up on the product. Chances are slim that when the mart runs out of stock, there will be another shipment anytime soon.

Therefore, Tamimi's rocks in Yasmin's humble opinion. Its regularity of shipments and variety of products can't be beat! She's in heaven when she sees the fresh mandarins, mangoes and dried chili peppers from Pakistan, plus the lentils and spices that are traditionally used in her culture. Although Yasmin's not a great cook, whenever she's homesick for Dahl, Haleem, Nihari, and Siri Paye, she can easily find the ingredients at Tamimi's and get busy preparing these comfort foods in her little kitchen. Conversely, if Yasmin doesn't feel like cooking, and yearns for traditional home-cooked meals, she's got the privilege of being able to purchase items from the Hot Foods section at Tamimi's. As far as she's concerned, their samosas and biryani dishes are absolutely scrummy!

There's even a Healthy Living department at Tamimi's for customers who want to buy natural, organic, and gluten-free products. Bee pollen and Bjorg brand soymilk from France, kale leaves from Holland, seaweed crackers from Japan, and everything else in between, can be found in this section. Understandably, the prices at Tamimi's are steep; therefore, Yasmin only buys things that would be considered luxury items: quinoa, real maple syrup, and raw honey, now and again as a treat, or when they are discounted. The Meat and Seafood sections are also first rate. Shoppers can buy camel, chicken, and lamb sourced from local farmers, fish imported from Egypt, and beef from Australia.

While the shopping at Tamimi's is fantastic, the thing that Yasmin loves most about her outings there is the opportunity to mingle with expats from all around the world. Although superficial, she enjoys this kind of social interaction. Making small talk with her sisters from the motherland while waiting in a queue to have their produce weighed and priced, makes Yasmin feel more connected and less lonely. She finds the rhythm of the Filipino language fascinating; so, she likes to listen to the loud exchanges between the Pinoys as they shop. Although Yasmin knows that they aren't quarreling, it always sounds like they're arguing to her.

Tamimi's is also quite popular with the locals. Therefore, the Arabic language swirls around her as Saudi families come out to shop. Yasmin's amazed at how much shopping the Saudis do. Their shopping carts are always piled high with Persil liquid detergents for their thobes and abayas, Laban, Sunflower cooking oil, ghee, Basmati rice, fava beans, hummus, khobz, plus assorted meats and pastries. As her mother would say, "they have enough food to feed an army."

The only negative thing that Yasmin has to say about her grocery shopping experience is the Saudis' tendency to cut queues. Actually, queue-cutting is her biggest shopping pet peeve in the Kingdom. It really miffs her when the Saudis cut in front of her and other expats. She's convinced that some of them must think that they are more important than members of the expat community. And others possibly believe that expats don't have anything better to do with their time than stand in a long queue for an eternity. As such, Yasmin always dreads getting stuck behind a Saudi who cuts in front of her. On one occasion, she almost threw a conniption when a Saudi couple cut in front of her with not one, but TWO shopping carts full of groceries. Ooh, was Yasmin furious! She had less than seven items in her basket. Anyhow, Saudis are not just guilty of this offense at Tamimi's, they have also conferred VIP status on themselves at other grocery shops, and establishments such as: pharmacies, post offices, and fast-food restaurants. It's just the way it is in the Kingdom.

A young Saudi woman cuts in front of Monica while she's placing her groceries on the checkout belt. *No, you don't lady! We're not going to play this to – day,* Monica thinks to herself. "La!" Monica said aloud as she tapped the offending woman on her left shoulder. "The end of the line is back there," she gestured with her right hand. "Sis – ter!" the Saudi woman begged... *Oh, now I'm your sister huh...a minute ago, I was invisible,* thought Monica. "Sis – ter, <u>look</u> only five things." Tired of the locals' habit of cutting in front of her and other expats, Monica is immune to the woman's pleas. Addressing the cashier, she said, "I'm next. Please start ringing up my purchases." Totally ignoring her "sister" Monica resumed placing her groceries on the belt.

"Yay, one for us expats!" A feminine, British voice said behind Monica. Grinning, Monica turned around to look at the speaker. She saw an olive complexioned woman standing two people behind her. From her features, she guessed that the woman was of Indian or Pakistani descent. They exchanged pleasantries. "Hi, I'm Yasmin." Monica shook her hand and replied, "I'm Monica. Nice to meet you." After paying her bill, Monica waited for Yasmin to finish her transaction at the checkout counter. "You look familiar," Yasmin told Monica. Monica vaguely recalled having seen Yasmin at Tamimi's on a few other occasions. "Well, I do shop here weekly," she replied.

"Me, too. Isn't it an awesome store?"

"It sure is. It's almost as good as Whole Foods Market back home."

"So, where's home for you?"

"New York City. And you?"

"Birmingham."

The women conversed in front of Tamimi's as they waited for their respective bus to arrive. Yasmin admired Monica's spunk and was getting good vibes from her. So, she said to her, "Listen, on Saturdays I get cracking in the kitchen and make some scrummy Pakistani dishes. You're welcome to join me anytime." "Thanks for the invite," Monica replied politely. "I do love Pakistani food." As their buses pulled into the parking lot, the women quickly exchanged cellphone numbers and promised to keep in touch with each other.

CHAPTER

8

W*ELL, I'M NOT THE FIRST woman to go through a separation from her man and I certainly won't be the last,* Pamela mumbled as she dialed her brother Lyle's telephone number. His phone rings three times before he answers it gruffly. It's midnight, who the devil could be calling at this hour? As soon as Lyle hears his sister's voice, his tone softens. "Pammy! What's up lil sis?"

Despite not seeing each other often, Lyle and Pamela are still very close. Weekly, they correspond via email, and speak with each other over the telephone at least once every month. Pamela's lengthy pause before replying caused her brother to stop surfing the TV channels. "Oh, nothing much," Pamela lied. "We haven't chatted in a while, so, I'm just calling to see how ya doing."

"At midnight?" Lyle replied in disbelief.

After another awkward silence, he pressed his sister for more information, "Pammy, what's going on? Surely, you didn't call at this hour just to shoot the breeze."

Pamela chuckled nervously, "You know me well, my brother. Anyhow, I was just thinking that we haven't seen each other in ages and a reunion is in order. As you know, for years I've wanted to take an Amtrak train ride across the U.S. Well, I'm finally gonna do it! I'm leaving Dhahran in a couple of weeks. My first stop will be Texas; then I'm gonna head out West to Portland, Oregon and then make my way to San Francisco. I'd love to see you if you're gonna be around."

Lyle listened intently to what his sister said and likewise, to what she didn't say. Choosing his words carefully, he replied, "Geez, Pammy, it's so unlike you to do something this big on the spur of the moment. I bet your decision has taken Glenn by surprise too."

Pamela had never been good at keeping secrets from her brother. Relieved to be able to drop the charade, she sighed heavily before leveling with Lyle. When she had finished saying her piece, she felt better. There was really no reason for her to have been embarrassed. Her brother is not the judgmental type. One thing that Pamela had always appreciated about Lyle was that she could always count on him to have her back – whether he agreed with her decisions or not.

CHAPTER

9

E XACTLY SIX MONTHS AFTER MY arrival in Riyadh, Khalid informed me that I would be dining with his mother at a traditional Saudi restaurant the following evening. I was a tad annoyed that he did not think to consult me first prior to scheduling this appointment with his mother. I'm, however, relieved that she would now be aware of my existence. At the appointed hour, I waited for them in front of the Najd Village. When I heard the purr of Khalid's Mercedes Cabriolet, my heart began to beat faster, and my palms became clammy. While he parked his convertible, I quickly wiped my hands on my abaya and tried to calm down.

Khalid made the necessary introductions and then excused himself. I noticed that he had inherited his huge, bright eyes from his mother. Everything about her carriage indicated that she defied social conventions. Her abaya, instead of being the standard drab, black, polyester garment, was a chic, black cotton cloak with alternating red and white buttons running down the middle. Furthermore, she wasn't wearing the niqab. I initially thought that she had forgotten it in Khalid's vehicle. So, I said, "Oh, Mrs. Abeer, you've forgotten your niqab."

"No dear, I never wear that thing," she replied contemptuously.

"Really, I thought that all females in the Kingdom must wear the niqab in public."

"I follow the teachings of the Holy Qur'an. There's no passage in it that states a woman must cover her face. Her hair - yes, but

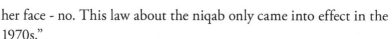

her face - no. This law about the niqab only came into effect in the 1970s."

"Don't the police harass you?"

"Sure, they do! Some of my Saudi sisters also try to pressure me into conforming, but I pay them absolutely no mind."

On that note, Mrs. Abeer swung the restaurant door open and walked briskly inside.

The Najd Village is a superb restaurant in Riyadh that's renowned for its delicious cuisine, ambience, and décor. While I had previously heard about The Village, this was my first-time dining here; and so, as Mrs. Abeer and I walked over to our reserved booth, I discreetly scanned the fine collection of antiquities adorning the walls and floor. Several of the waiters greeted her with warmth, deference, and familiarity, so I realized that she was a regular client.

From my brief exchange with Mrs. Abeer outside the restaurant, I felt that I was in the presence of a kindred free spirit and immediately took a liking to her. Her sassiness and strength of character intrigued me. Like her son, Mrs. Abeer was born in Riyadh and educated in London. She was, by profession, an artist; and owned an art gallery in the heart of Riyadh. Since Saudi women of Mrs. Abeer's generation were not allowed to own and operate businesses, Mrs. Abeer registered her gallery under her father's name. Even after marrying Khalid's father, Dr. Mahmood - who was a diplomat, and becoming a mother, Mrs. Abeer continued to paint and travel abroad, exhibiting her creations in London, New York, and Paris.

When we reached our booth, she daintily sat cross-legged on the plush, red, handwoven Bedouin rug which boasted an intricate pattern of black triangles and white squares. Graciously, she accepted the cup of coffee that the waiter poured her out of an antique copper coffee pot. Upon hearing that this was my first-time dining at The Village, Mrs. Abeer suggested that I try the restaurant's house specialty – moqalqal (peppery lamb) and matazzez (Saudi dumplings). And so, I dutifully ordered those dishes.

When our food was served, we got down to business. I had expected Mrs. Abeer to interview me about my engagement to Khalid and ask probing questions about my proficiency at performing certain wifely duties. Instead, she made inquiries about four things: my readiness to marry into her family and culture, my family's view of the union, my Arabic lessons, and plans to resume my career. I suspect that she is the exception to the rule of Saudi mothers where the evaluation of potential candidates for the position of daughter-in-law is concerned. Anyhow, I was quite frank in my response to her questions: Yes, despite cultural differences, I'm committed to Khalid and feel comfortable living in Riyadh. No, I haven't told my family about him, yet. My Arabic conversation lessons are going well, thank you, but the writing class is a tad challenging. Presently, I don't have any immediate plans to revive my career, but when I do, I hope to be as successful as you in balancing family and career. Mrs. Abeer beamed at my compliment. Then she delicately wiped her mouth and fingers on a cotton napkin, and said, "Good! I'm happy to hear these things. Next week Saturday morning, we're going to get you fitted for your wedding dress. You and Khalid will marry this September after Eid Al Adha."

Later that night, I happily relayed to Khalid - over the telephone - the conversation that I had earlier on with his mother. He laughed heartily and said, "Congrats my love, on passing her test." Feeling confident, as soon as my call with Khalid ended, I dialed my parents' number. There was an awkward silence after I delivered my good news to them. Although in my heart of hearts I didn't expect that my parents would be thrilled with my decision to marry a Saudi, a part of me still somehow hoped they would be happy for my happiness. My delusion became evident when shortly thereafter, I heard a click and the phone's dial tone. Slowly, I put the telephone receiver down. Understandably, this was a huge shock for my parents. So, I thought it best to give them time to process my breaking news before contacting them again.

CHAPTER

10

ALHAMDULILLAH, I'VE SURVIVED THE PROBATIONARY period at this bloody start-up college. It wasn't easy with all the disorganization, lack of vision and resources at the institution, plus the rife malcontent of the staff. Several colleagues couldn't cope with the ongoing situation of teaching without textbooks, having limited classroom supplies, and/or having to sit on the filthy floor because the classroom furniture still hadn't arrived. So, they went quietly into the good night. By nature, I'm not a quitter, I like to finish what I've started, but it's becoming increasingly challenging to stay the course. Moreover, there had been a spate of thefts at my workplace. Several admins and teachers - including yours truly - had snacks, jewelry, and cash, mysteriously vanish from office desks, or handbags. I'm still sore about my large pack of McVitie's digestives being nicked. The crook could have had the decency to leave me with a few biscuits.

Anyhow, each day brought a fresh round of aggravation and morale was very low. There was a lot of bitching and undermining by staff as teachers tried to secure their jobs. That's not who I am as a person; so, I kept my colleagues at arm's length. And tried to stay under the radar as I went about my business.

Subsequently, however, I had formed an alliance of sorts with another teacher. Her name's Lydia and she's Asian-Canadian. She's very private. So, I didn't know much about her, or why she came to Saudi Arabia. All I know is that she's from Canada and teaches the upper-intermediate English students. Like me, Lydia liked to lounge by the swimming pool on our compound after work. She was very predictable. She could always be found reclined on a chaise lounge, wearing her signature wide-brimmed Burberry sun hat. She usually had her headphones on; so, I took it that she didn't want to be disturbed. Therefore, prior to lowering myself in the chaise next to Lydia's, I would acknowledge her with a smile. Then, I'd spend the next hour reading a self-improvement book on my Kindle. Our routine continued like this for several weeks, before Lydia spoke to me.

I remembered that afternoon very well. We had just endured another long, pointless staff meeting. I say pointless because we were always asked for ideas on how to improve the operations of the organization, told how great our ideas were, and then nothing came of them. So, why waste our time with this bollocks? The only worthwhile thing that came out of that meeting was the information about some big, upcoming inspection. All hell broke loose – talk about a kerfuffle! I felt a little badly for the dean, as many teachers were venting quite disrespectfully about the short deadline and additional paperwork that must be done before the inspectors arrived. My peers were right to be royally ticked off. We were already stretched to the max. Instead of getting better, things were getting worse. Everybody was stressed and buckling under the strain. Personally speaking, I was beginning to question myself, the wisdom of staying the course. Yes, I understood that this was a start-up, and of course, things would be a bit rough in the beginning, but my duties were becoming increasingly outrageous and burdensome. I was hired as a Learning Coach, for crying out loud. However, instead, I was really working as a full-time teacher and not being fairly compensated in return.

On one occasion when Lydia and I were lounging by the lovely swimming pool, she remarked to me, "This job is like being in a bad marriage. You see that the relationship is unhealthy, yet you hang in there hoping that it will get better." She cracked me up! Despite the seriousness of the matter, I burst out laughing. Although

I had never been married, I too was beginning to feel as if I was married to the job. In addition to putting in the contracted forty hours at the college, we were also working at least twenty hours extra at the compound on a weekly basis without any additional compensation. As such, I could see both the truth and humor in what Lydia had said. I liked her wit! Now that the ice had thawed, I felt a connection to her. Listen, we were in the minority here - the only two staff members of Asian heritage - and therefore, we needed to band together. So, although Lydia wasn't Muslim, and we were from different environments, I still felt that she was my sister. I noticed that Lydia doesn't wear a wedding ring. I'm curious about her marital status, but don't want to pry. Is she married? Separated? Divorced? From Lydia's comment, it's possible that she was speaking from personal experience. Perhaps, as our relationship evolved, I'd get to the bottom of this mystery.

CHAPTER
11

*H*OW CAN FEMALE WESTERNERS LIVE *in the Kingdom for years?* Monica wondered as she reflected on all the madness and aggravation surrounding her. She was finding it quite difficult to adjust to the restrictive Saudi lifestyle long-term. Everything was just so unnecessarily complicated. For instance, when she went shopping at the malls and wanted to try on an outfit, she was forced to eye ball it because clothing stores are bereft of fitting rooms. Heaven forbid, if Monica purchased some clothes and needed to return them, she only had two days to do so. This was a bit inconvenient, since the compound bus only took teachers to the malls on specific days each week. So, in the event she needed to make a return on a day there was no bus trip, she would have to reserve a taxi to transport her to and from the mall. For safety reasons, female expats were strongly cautioned against riding in taxis alone. So, Monica would then have to find a colleague who was willing to accompany her to and from the mall. This was problematic, because her colleague might not value time the way she does. Monica was a real stickler for punctuality. And got bent out of shape when her peers were tardy in returning to the bus after a shopping trip. While she could excuse them being late a few minutes, when the same teachers were habitually fifteen minutes late, she began to take their behavior personally. Therefore, the matter of finding a reliable travel buddy posed its own set of challenges.

Anyhow, getting back to the issue of clothes shopping, Monica had recently purchased two skirts that needed to be altered. One was a size too big, the other was too long. Since alteration services aren't available at the malls, women must find a tailor. As luck would have it, the closest one to Monica's residence was twenty minutes travel distance (one way) by vehicle. So, one afternoon, she contacted one of the taxi drivers who was regularly used by her peers and made the trip.

Due to social conduct laws, women weren't permitted to enter tailor shops. Therefore, Monica stood at the door and handed her clothes to the Indian tailor. The way the man reluctantly took her garments from her, ensuring that his fingers didn't touch hers, made her feel like a social pariah. It was as if she had some contagious disease. Anyhow, he in turn, guesstimated how much tailoring needed to be done and altered her skirts. After collecting her clothes from the tailor, Monica returned to her abode, with fingers crossed, and hoped they would fit properly. Too complicated!

Last weekend, Monica bought a beautiful skirt on sale that was almost perfect – except that it was too big in the waist. Rather than deal with the hassle of taking it to the tailor, whenever she wanted to wear the skirt, she simply folded over the waist and secured it with a bull clip. Problem solved.

A bigger headache for Monica, however, was the issue of dining out. It pained her to see the *Gents Only* sign posted by the door or window of a lovely restaurant that she'd like to dine at. By nature, she's very fond of spicy food and there were some great Indian and Pakistani restaurants nearby her compound. Unfortunately, if she wanted to order something, she must ask a male colleague to do the honors. Monica was lucky that one of her American peers frequently dined at these eateries and was kind enough to bring her back a dish.

Although she's not keen on junk food, she would occasionally buy some because fast food restaurants have a section for families and likewise, singles. Call Monica naïve, but when she first arrived, she thought that the Singles section was for unmarried people. Hah! It turned out that it is only for men who were unaccompanied by their families. Monica learned this the hard way one afternoon when she tried to order a Happy Meal at Burger King. She had just finished walking around the perimeter of the corniche and fancied a bite to eat. Therefore, she stopped at Burger King for lunch. She noticed that the Families section was crowded, but the Singles section was empty. So, since she's not married, she attempted to place her order in the Singles section.

As soon as Monica put her foot in the door, the Filipino employee made a big ruckus.

"Madam, you need to go to the Families section."

"But, I'm single," she protested.

"Madam, you cannot come inside. This section is only for men," the worker replied quite sternly.

"But there's nobody here. I just want to order a Happy Meal," Monica pleaded.

"No, madam. You <u>must</u> go to the Families section."

"Sir, the queues in the Families section are very long. Why can't you just serve me?"

Monica's pleas fell on deaf ears; the counter server threatened to call the manager if she didn't leave. While she understood the man's fear about getting in trouble for breaking the law, she was still miffed. The time that he had spent ordering her to go to the Families section was longer than the time it would have taken him to prepare her food. Judging from the length of the lines in the Families section, Monica figured it would be better for her to continue her journey home. She would arrive home long before the Happy Meal would be ready. So, she scrapped her original plan for lunch and quickly exited the Singles section.

As for the subject of hair care – let's not even go THERE. The salons in the Kingdom don't cater to clients with Black hair. So, Monica had to go to Bahrain for hair appointments. Thank God, it was just an hour's drive away. In Manama, there were several East African hairdressers who would cut and style her hair just right. If Monica wanted, she could also get her hair braided just like her grand-ma used to do it when she was a child.

While the disadvantages far outweighed the advantages, Monica confessed that some of the restrictions had been very beneficial to her. For starters, banking was a breeze. The lines in the Ladies' section of the banks were always much shorter than those in the Gents' section. The only time that she could recall the women's line being as long as the men's was when the bank ran out of cash. That's right – completely out of riyals. Then all customers sat around for a couple of hours - in segregated areas naturally - waiting for the main branch to deliver some currency. Monica noticed that this cash shortage tended to occur at crucial times. For instance, Ramadan, Eid, and college mid-semester breaks. Now that she was wise to this issue, she withdrew a little extra cash each month, so she wouldn't be in a bind during a major holiday season.

Where the wearing of the abaya is concerned, Monica was in the minority in her enthusiasm for it. While women might be split in their views over having to wear the abaya, they would all probably concede that there were two significant benefits to wearing this garment: the saving of time and money. Take for an instance, the act of shaving. Since no one would see their legs, women didn't have to bother shaving. Therefore, it was unnecessary to purchase tubes of Nair.

Another perk was having the freedom to wear whatever outfit they felt like wearing in public under their abaya. Hence, women could go to work in their sportswear, or pajamas for that matter if they pleased, and no one would be the wiser.

Now, while Monica adored her abaya, she admitted that the niqab and her didn't get on. As a matter of fact, she resented having to wear it. In general, she loathed synthetic fabrics and had nothing to do with them back in the USA. So, being required to wear the niqab, which was made from polyester, was a huge hassle for her.

CHAPTER

12

"HONEY, YOU CAN'T COUNT ON a man's financial support," Pamela's mother had warned her when she broke the news of her engagement. "Promise me that you will put a lil something aside for your financial security in an individual account," she had pleaded. Recalling her mother's words, Pamela could kick herself. Being confident about her future with Glenn, she had never bothered to open an individual savings account, or concerned herself with investing. While berating herself, an idea flashed across her mind. Warming to it, a wisp of a smile tugged at the corners of her lips.

Later that night, Pamela squashed the guilt that attempted to prick her conscience. *Heck, if Glenn had upheld his end of the bargain, I wouldn't have to resort to deception,* she told herself. After taking a couple of deep breaths to steady her nerves, she calmly marched into the den. As usual, Glenn was hunched over some building blueprints. Lightly, Pamela began to massage his neck and shoulders. "Sugar," she cooed, "I saw several absolutely daahling dresses at Al Rashid Mall that would be perfect for our upcoming trip to Bhutan. However, they cost a bit more than my monthly allowance I'm afraid," she sighed heavily.

By nature, Glenn was a generous man. Moreover, he prided himself in his ability to provide for his wife's material needs. However, this pride wasn't merely about stroking his ego. Glenn genuinely loved making Pamela happy. After all, she was a wonderful woman and quite charming. Covering both of her hands with his own, he

48

squeezed them gently and said, "Princess, as an early birthday gift from me, why don't you go on a shopping spree?" Releasing Pamela's hands, Glenn pulled his debit card from his wallet and handed it to her. Promptly, she withdrew several thousand dollars from the ATM on their compound. Afterwards, she felt ashamed of herself. She had never thought highly of manipulative women; or ever imagined that she would join their rank one day. But, as Mindy McCready used to sing, "A Girl's Gotta Do, What A Girl's Gotta Do." The wheels were now in motion and there was no turning back.

CHAPTER

13

'M ON A MISSION. AN ambitious one I might add, to balance the scales of reporting on life in the Kingdom. Media reports about life in Saudi Arabia are usually negative, so I'm on a mission to showcase the positive via my travel blog. Like every other country, Saudi Arabia - believe it or not - also has its share of fascinating sights. For instance, history buffs will delight in the wonders of Al Dir'iya near Riyadh, and the Nabatean's military outpost base in Made'in Al Saleh near Madinah; or marvel at the 9,000-year-old rock drawings at Jubbah. Intrepid adventurers can go camping in the Empty Quarter, or hike to the Edge of the World. Lovers of architecture will enjoy a boat ride to Farasan Island to view the Ottoman architecture; roaming through Jeddah's historic district which is full of colorful doors, and some magnificent former sea merchants' homes.

Several months ago, the Saudi Minister of Tourism was heavily criticized when he commented that the Kingdom - when it becomes open for tourism - will not be for the backpacker type of tourist. In his defense, I must say this is indeed the case. To get to these destinations from Riyadh, a train ride, plane ride, and/or 4x4 vehicle is required. Then, one must also budget for lodging, meals, and sometimes entrance fees. On average, an overnight trip can easily end up costing a traveler $400 USD. Therefore, most expats from Africa and Asia are, unfortunately, automatically excluded from physically enjoying these places.

There are several reputable tour companies in Riyadh that cater to expats and provide English-speaking tour guides. So, if Khalid and I didn't have plans for any given weekend, I usually joined one of their tours. In addition to learning more about Saudi Arabia's rich heritage, these outings were a nice way for me to meet fellow expats, many of whom were American or British. When I mentioned that I'm engaged to a Saudi, they were usually surprised. I totally understood this; as previously stated, I too was surprised by this unexpected twist in my life's trajectory. Anyhow, while I can accept people's shock, I have little tolerance for their narrow-mindedness. So, things got ugly quickly on a recent tour that I took to the Heritage Mud Village in Al Ghat city.

On the trip, I sat next to another solo female traveler. If memory serves me correctly, her name was Yasmin. I recalled that she was from Birmingham, UK. Since she and I had several things in common: age, profession, and religion, we were getting on just fine. Until I revealed that my fiancé was a Saudi. It all started when she admired my 22-karat tri-color gold engagement ring.

"Oh, what a gorgeous ring!"

"Thank you. I recently got engaged."

"Congratulations! The combination of the rose with white and yellow gold is just brilliant – very unique."

"Thanks. My fiancé and I also had our initials engraved on the interior."

"How lovely! If you don't mind me asking, where did you buy your ring?"

"Al-Fardan's Jewelry Store."

"Ooh, Al-Fardan's! I sometimes window shop at their Al-Khobar location."

"I love Al-Khobar. Is that where you live?"

"Yes, it is. So, how is your fiancé coping with life in the Kingdom?"

"Uhm… he's a Saudi National."

Well, it's a good thing that looks can't kill because she shot me the evilest of looks! While several passersby looked daggers at Khalid and me in London, I was still taken aback by her reaction. So, I said in as pleasant a tone as I could muster, "You're acting as if I'm guilty of committing a heinous crime." She stared at me coldly, before replying, "Well, I'm not surprised that you are marrying a Saudi. Your kind makes good trophy wives."

I cannot tell a lie, her words stung deeply. And put a damper on my mood for the rest of the tour. Prior to her comment, she had seemed like such a nice woman. She was the last person I had expected to throw shade on me. So I thought it best to put some distance between her and me. I stood up and told her, "For the record, my Khalid is no sugar daddy. It so happens that he's the same age as us." Then I walked to the center of the bus where there was a vacant seat. I tried hard not to let her mean comment bother me, and reminded myself that what other people thought about me was not my business – that was their business. Whether I appreciated their sentiments or not, ultimately, they were entitled to their opinions.

Yes, I knew that being blonde and blue-eyed was an asset in the Middle East - and other parts of the world for that matter. Yes, I was well aware that women who looked like me received privileges based solely on appearance. However, I shouldn't be crucified, or made to feel that I owe the world an apology. I have no control over my appearance or heritage. None of us do. We all get what we get and must make the best of it. While it's sad that the foundation of some marriages is based on physical characteristics, I'd like to think that Khalid is not so superficial, and there is more to our relationship than my physical features.

Anyhow, I digress. Back to the business about why I started a travel blog. This decision wasn't an easy one to make. Keeping in mind my location and the censorship on speech, I initially balked at the idea of blogging. As you might be aware, a young, male Saudi blogger was sentenced to 10 years in prison and 1,000 lashes for setting up a website that advocated free speech in the Kingdom. There was also the case of an English expat woman, who incidentally, happened to be married to a Saudi, having her website shut down by the Saudi government because of its "offensive" content. Nevertheless, since I've always enjoyed writing and the tension between words, I thought that blogging would be a productive use of my free time. My blog would be a harmless, free publicity tool for the Kingdom. Therefore, I decided to run my idea by Khalid. I'm pleased to report that he was very supportive of my plan; but cautioned me to blog under a pseudonym. And so, dear reader, that was the genesis of "A Swede in Riyadh" travel blog.

Books, Travel, and Writing have been my constant companions since childhood. Perhaps this was a result of my being an only child? I'm not sure. All I know is that I've always enjoyed reading about exotic places, going on trips, and journaling. This might be the reason why I had five pen-friends scattered across the globe by my thirteenth birthday. There was Yumiko in Tokyo, Joseph in Ghana, Lenora in Denver, Helen in Belfast and Chris in Perth. Oh, how I looked forward to checking the mailbox each afternoon back then. Often, I'd wait impatiently for the mailman's arrival with anticipation of receiving a letter from one of my pals.

Family and school outings to local parks and museums were also a lot of fun. I recall how I used to pen my thoughts about an upcoming adventure, in my diary. It was of great sentimental value to me because my mother had lovingly knitted the cover. Anyhow, after the trip, I would again write about the highlights in my diary. To this day, whenever I travel, I still jot down a few things that strike me about a place that I've visited and take tons of photos.

Since photography is prohibited in most public spaces around Saudi Arabia, I depended heavily on both my memory and journal for information about my adventures around the Kingdom. Despite a dearth of images, I'm proud to say that my blog was still quite popular with expats. Several followers even contacted me regularly for more information about visiting places in and around Riyadh that are off the beaten path. Helping fellow expats unravel the

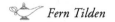

enigma that shrouds Saudi Arabia has made me feel good about my blog.

Recently, the Saudi government lifted the ban on female students using their cellphones at school. Who knows, the day might soon come when the prohibition of photography in most public spaces will also be lifted.

CHAPTER
14

YASMIN'S PATIENCE WITH HER MATHEMATICS students was beginning to wear thin. With a stern look and voice to match, she said, "Come on, girls. You're taking a test. The next person I catch cheating is going to get a zero!" She walked up and down the rows with her eagle eyes darting left and right, daring the students to defy her order. One of the things that Yasmin found peculiar about the Saudi students is that they don't consider cheating or "helping" each other - as they prefer to call it - on their tests haram. Along the same lines, she found it comical in a wry sense that they would also ask teachers to "help them" when they were being tested. *Cheeky buggers,* Yasmin thought to herself, as she suppressed a smile.

A few minutes later, she scowled at a student who was craning her neck to see the answers of the girl seated in front of her. As Yasmin walked towards the offender, the girl quickly averted her eyes. Towering over the student, Yasmin made the traditional Arabic tut sound of disapproval and exclaimed, "La! Fatimah, this is your last warning. Go sit at my desk and finish writing your test." Fatimah prudently avoided eye contact with Yasmin and meekly did as she was told.

Shortly thereafter, Yasmin glanced at her watch. She was relieved to see that it was almost time to end the test. "You've got five minutes left – FIVE minutes," she announced to the class. For clarity, she also wrote the number 5 on the easel. After Yasmin had collected the last test paper, she grudgingly put them in her tote bag. She was not looking forward to grading these papers later at the compound. *This is absolute bollocks!* she fumed as she hoisted her bag on her left shoulder. All this covering of other teachers' classes was getting out of control and beginning to take a toll on her. When Yasmin accepted the position of Learning Coach, it was because she didn't want to be a regular teacher. She had no interest in assuming all the responsibilities that full-time teachers did. Now, practically every day, she had to cover a class because a teacher called in sick or jumped ship. If it wasn't Mathematics, it was English. If it wasn't English, it was IT. To add insult to injury, the dean made it clear that there would be no overtime pay for all these additional teaching hours and duties. Come the new trimester, if Yasmin continued to have this heavy workload, she was going to request that the dean change her job title to EFL instructor and compensate her in kind for her services.

CHAPTER

15

MONICA WAS SO GLAD THAT she had made the effort to get to know Lauren. She had been a huge source of support and wisdom for her. Without Lauren's friendship, it would have been even more challenging for Monica to cope with the politics and lunacy of their workplace. Monica doesn't know how Lauren managed it all, but in addition to teaching, she was currently taking two courses online and steadily working towards a master's degree in Social Work. Monica really admired Lauren's drive and tried not to impose on her personal time too much.

While neither of them were big on bonding by nature, they did get together after work in the middle of each week for a little girl talk. Being a typical Southerner, Lauren always prepared some tea and snacks whenever she was the host. Her ritual was to first pour Monica and herself a cup of tea. Next, she would curl up in her usual spot on the sofa. Only then did the pals begin their tête-à-tête.

"I don't know about you Lauren, but I thought it was a bit harsh of management to terminate Marla just because she told her students that they needed to wear deodorant," Monica remarked on one occasion.

"I told you," Lauren replied, "these girls are vicious and run the show here. Anyhow, I think that there was more to their decision to terminate Marla than meets the eye. I feel that the deodorant snafu, though, was the straw that broke the camel's back."

"Wow, you've really got to mind your Ps and Qs around here."

Lauren offered Monica some Danish butter cookies and she took two. While nibbling on one of them, Monica asked, "What do you make of this, Lauren? Yesterday, I had to cover Yolanda's class because she was out sick. When we returned to the compound, I stopped by her apartment to see how she was feeling and she just gave me a weird look." Lauren smirked, "Honey, I'm not surprised. I know for a FACT that she wasn't really sick. She told me herself that she was absent from work because she had a terrible hangover." Monica arched her eyebrow and sighed loudly. "Are you serious? Lauren, I could have done without that info! That was very uncool of Yolanda. I expected better from her. What kind of people are we working with?" Lauren chuckled, "Yeah, this place is a real circus. Lots of clowns and buffoons. I have a feeling that all of this is going to blow up in their faces. And I don't want to be here when the you-know-what hits the fan."

Three days earlier, Lauren had mentioned to Monica that she had seen an ad listed on Craigslist, Saudi Arabia, by an expat who had household items for sale.

"So, are you going to check out the stuff?" Monica asked her.

"Hell, yeah! Even if I don't buy anything, it gives me a good excuse to visit the Salam Camp and see how the oil expats live." The women both laughed.

"Well, if you'd like some company, I'll go with you," Monica offered.

"I'd like that," Lauren replied. "There's strength in numbers and you can never be too sure about some people who post on Craigslist. Oh, just for giggles, I also peeped at the Personals section. My Lord, do we have a lot of lonely and kinky men in the Kingdom!"

"Considering all the restrictions on personal liberty here, that doesn't surprise me."

CHAPTER

16

GLENN SMILED HIS APPROVAL AS Pamela modeled for him the eight designer outfits that she had purchased at the mall. While many women Pamela's age struggled to remain trim, her svelte figure naturally defied gravity. She continued to wear a size 6 dress, just as she did at university. Except for crow's feet, her face was naturally free from wrinkles. As she twirled, Glenn made a mental note to stop by Joyalukkas jewelry store. On his last trip there, he had spied a pair of baguette diamond 22-karat gold earrings, which would be the perfect complement for Pamela's new clothes.

Two days later, Pamela went back to the mall and returned her fabulous garments. Despite her ability to justify her actions, she still felt guilty about requesting a store refund. Carefully she put the thick wad of cash in her purse, and zipped her bag shut. Then she cheerfully bid the store clerk a good day and left the mall.

When she arrived home, she sorted through her clothes closet bursting with her favorite designers: Carolina Herrera, Emilio Pucci, and Ralph Rucci. The time had come for her to decide which to sell, keep, or leave behind. She winced when she saw some dresses with their price tags still affixed. Others had only been worn once or twice. Pamela wondered, when did she become such a clothes horse? After sorting her outfits into three piles, she spent the next hour dialing her pals who wore her dress size. And informed them of her clothes for sale. "Honey," she gushed, "when your wardrobe doors can't shut, you know that it's time to downsize."

She felt no need to tell them the real reason for her sale. Although these ladies and Pamela had been friendly for years, she didn't really consider them her friends. As far as she was concerned, they were simply nice people to socialize with while living in this inhospitable land. If the time ever arose when they were summonsed to testify in court, none of them could provide intimate details about Pamela. At best, all that any of them could say, was that she was a gracious hostess, who hosted elegant parties at her refined villa. And that's the way Pamela preferred it to be. After recording in her Blackberry each woman's appointment time to view her outfits, Pamela turned her attention to her jewelry.

She reached for the black, mother-of-pearl lacquerware box that housed her special occasion pieces. Carefully, she opened the lid of the box and admired her treasures. Thanks to her husband, she had amassed a fine collection of 22-karat gold and platinum jewelry from Saudi Arabia, India, and Turkey. Lovingly, Pamela caressed each item. Although she loved them all, she knew that sentiment must take a back seat to practicality. With a critical eye, she appraised each object separately. While the Indian and Saudi jewelry pieces were stunning, they were also rather ornate. So, Pamela decided to sell them. Texans in general liked everything big and flashy; therefore, she would have no problem finding wealthy clients to purchase her bling.

Next, she studied her prized gems. They included: a platinum lion's head cocktail ring with ruby eyes – it had been a wedding anniversary gift; a lovely pair of sapphire flower earrings that had been a birthday present; a magnificent emerald pendant, and likewise a Swarovski blue butterfly brooch – both of which had been consolation gifts. Pamela picked up each piece of jewelry and held it to the sunlight. As the sun's rays hit the gems from various angles, she marveled at the craftsmanship.

Reflecting on her pre-Saudi Arabia self, Pamela giggled when she thought about the joy she had once felt from her humble collection of sterling silver and 18-karat gold jewelry. Boy, had she come a long way. Today, such dinky trinkets would not do – they weren't even fit to be worn by her around the house when she was home alone. Smiling wryly, Pamela reluctantly admitted to herself that Glenn wasn't the only one who had changed. She sighed heavily, as she pondered which of her treasures to keep and which to sell. Finally, she decided to sell all her consolation gifts. It was the only sensible thing for her to do. Why should she torment herself with these painful reminders of the reason why her marriage had disintegrated?

CHAPTER

17

SEVERAL WEEKS AFTER MY INITIAL call to my parents, I telephoned them again. Their answering machine came on. I told it how sorry I was to have broken the news about my engagement to them in that manner. I also mentioned how wonderful Khalid and Mrs. Abeer were and my belief that when my parents have had the opportunity to meet them, they would agree with my sentiments. I promised to call again next month and ended by saying how much I loved and missed them.

The following weeks were very busy as Mrs. Abeer and I planned my nuptials. I don't know how I would have managed if she wasn't so kind and supportive. There were numerous appointments with the wedding planner, hair stylist, henna artist, florists, caterers and seamstress. While it was a very exciting time, it was also very stressful for me; especially since I was not Saudi and was still in the process of adjusting to this unique culture. As you may have gathered, things were done differently in this country. So, I tried my best not to get too flustered when things didn't go as quickly, or as smoothly as I would have liked them to. More importantly, I was learning to relax and leave everything in Mrs. Abeer's capable hands.

As promised, the next month, I dialed my parents' number at the time they and I usually talked. Once again, their answering machine came on. While I was leaving my message, I had the eerie feeling that my parents were right there screening my call. I could picture them in their spacious living room filled with treasured family heirlooms. My mother, curled up on the sky-blue Gustavian couch that she had inherited from her maternal grandmother. If she wasn't knitting, she was flipping through books of knitting patterns. While my father would be in his customary seat - a 19C Rococo claw-foot chair that had once belonged to his great uncle, Ingvar - to the right of the marble fireplace, warming his body.

While I was relaying the information about the status of my wedding preparations, a voice that sounded like my mother's interfered. I say it sounded like hers, because it lacked her usual warmth and happiness. This voice that sounded like my mother's was quite hollow and cool. Politely, it said to me, "Inga, how could you <u>do</u> this to us? We are terribly disappointed with you. Please, don't call us anymore." And then the line went dead.

I tried my best to make sense of what had just transpired, and how it was possible that it had happened, but could not. As I attempted to reconcile the contradictions between the alien voice recently at the other end of the telephone line, and the familiar one of my liberal, maverick mother, who repeatedly voiced to me as a child and teenager that, "Love knows no boundaries." "You can't love people if you judge them." And, "It doesn't matter who you love, it only matters that you love," I became both angry and sad.

Part of me was tempted to dial my parents' number again, and express to them my disappointment with them. I wanted to bawl them out for being hypocrites and liars. I wanted to refresh their memories of their former teachings of, "We are all one." And ask them why they were now singing a totally different tune?

On the other hand, there was a part of me that wanted to reason with them. I wanted to inform them that their disappointment with me was misplaced. Contrary to their belief, I wasn't marrying some savage still living in the Stone Age. I was going to marry a cultured man who was literally a gentleman and a scholar. My union with Khalid would bring honor to our family – not disgrace.

In the end, I decided to respect the wishes of that distant voice which now emanated from my mother's mouth. I understood that my parents had fallen prey to the rise in Islamophobia that was afflicting Europe. The fear, distrust, and anger of Arabs and Muslims gripping many Europeans, had resulted in their hearts hardening, close-mindedness, and cynicism. As such, I couldn't really blame my parents for their behavior.

Perhaps it was wishful thinking on my part, but I found some measure of comfort in the fact that not all channels of communication between them and I were closed. While I was instructed not to call them anymore, I wasn't explicitly told that I couldn't contact them via e-mail. So, after the wedding, I planned to rekindle our relationship by e-mailing them some photos of my special day.

Mrs. Abeer is one remarkable woman! When I confessed to her that my parents didn't take the news about my wedding too well, she was very sympathetic. "Oh Inga, this must be such a difficult time for you," she said. "If you ever want to talk, don't hesitate to call me." While I appreciated Mrs. Abeer's offer and we were almost family, I didn't feel comfortable unburdening my problems on her. So, instead, I took solace and refuge in my journal. I wrote down all my angst over the current state of my relationship with my parents. I journaled about my confusion over the matter. In the process, I ended up writing a letter to them. I expressed myself fully about how they had hurt my feelings; conversely, I apologized for any pain that I had inflicted on them. I ended my letter optimistically. I told my parents that if they couldn't bring themselves to love Khalid and his family, I hoped that with time, they would at least be able to accept them. All this journaling was therapeutic; by the time I signed the letter with my usual "Love, XOXO" I felt better. Of course, I had no intention of sending this letter to my parents. Frankly speaking, I don't think that they would have been emotionally ready to receive it. Since this wasn't the type of letter that I would want others to stumble on by accident and read, I ended up burning it.

CHAPTER

18

YASMIN STRETCHED LAZILY ON THE couch and smiled at nothing in particular in her living room. It was Friday, and time for her to decompress and relax. After completing Salat al-Fajr (morning prayers), she loved to treat herself to a nice bowl of Alpen Muesli and catch up on the news. This morning, however, after reading a certain headline, Yasmin lost her appetite and felt her blood begin to boil. *Indian Maid's Right Hand Chopped Off by Her Saudi Employer*, announced the headline. Yasmin put her cereal bowl down and read the article. She read about the maid losing her hand because she complained about being overworked and underpaid, and literally felt sick to her stomach. With her breakfast threatening to dislodge itself, she rushed as fast as she could to the toilet.

Once her stomach settled, Yasmin got up and washed her cereal bowl. Still feeling weak, she collapsed on her sofa, and covered her face with her arm. *This abuse and exploitation of Asian workers has got to stop,* she said to herself. It was just two months ago that the expat community was in an uproar when the news broke that an Indonesian domestic worker had been repeatedly raped by her Saudi employer before being beaten to death. Now this - Yasmin wished that the Indian government would follow the lead of the Philippines government which ceased sending its citizens to Kuwait after several Pinoys working there committed suicide, and a housemaid's body - which showed signs of her having been tortured and strangled - was found stuffed in the freezer at her former employer's home. But, she knew that was highly unlikely. Poverty was rampant on the subcontinent and jobs in the Middle East were the only hope her less fortunate brothers and sisters had for supporting themselves and their families. So, despite the slave-like conditions under which they toiled for the pittance they earned, many of them still thought that it was worth their while to come to this region.

Yasmin was friendly with some of the Indian laborers on the compound and was shocked to learn that they worked twelve hours a day, six days a week, lived together in a cramped dormitory room, and had to work two full years before they were eligible for 30 days of unpaid leave. What was worse, many of them were still financially indebted to recruiter agents in their homeland for the privilege of coming to the Kingdom to eke out a meager living under such deplorable work conditions.

There was a real pecking order in the Kingdom. In general, the Egyptians were hired as doctors and pharmacists, while the Filipinas worked as nurses in the hospitals and clinics. Americans and Western Europeans were employed as educators, or engineers in the oil and manufacturing sectors. The Sudanese (and other Africans), Indonesian/Sri Lankan/Indian and Pakistani employees were primarily hired as domestic workers and construction laborers. It was an open secret that Westerners - Caucasians in particular - received the best treatment and benefits. In contrast, African and Asian people tended to get the menial jobs and were at the bottom of the dung heap. They were considered sub-human, had fewer rights, and were merely viewed as commodities. This wasn't surprising when one considered that slavery in the Kingdom was only abolished in 1962.

Although Yasmin was educated and came from a good family, it didn't mean squat in this region. She was still regarded with contempt. And she knew it. As she rolled over on to her side, she shuddered at the thought of what her life might have been like if her father hadn't made the decision to emigrate to London. Breaking free from the shackles of poverty, he had done very well for his family.

Neither his wife nor children wanted for anything. His relatives who still resided in Karachi also received financial assistance from him. Thanks to his self-sacrifices, Yasmin would never be subjected to the more horrific abuses of her less fortunate compatriots. She was in the Kingdom by design, out of a sense of adventure, not out of economic necessity. Grateful for her good fortune and overcome by emotion, she picked up the phone and rang home.

CHAPTER

19

*J*ESUS, SAVIOR, PILOT ME! GIVE *me the strength to deal with these provincial Saudis whose concept and standard of women are the Kardashian sisters...Dear Lord, please open their eyes to the fact that women across the globe come in different shapes and sizes. Amen!* Monica prayed silently. She just had what should have been a pleasant outing marred by a very ugly incident. Since relocating to Saudi Arabia, she had fallen in love with dates and begun to feast on them. The Medjool dates from Jordan were her favorite, but the local Khalas and Mabroom ran a close second. The Al-Qassim region of the Kingdom was renowned for its date farms. So, Monica took a trip there the weekend of the annual Dates Festival. Since the people in that province were rather conservative, she wore both her niqab and hijab.

Monica roamed the grounds enjoying the hustle and bustle of the festival. The popular event was teeming with locals, expats, and visitors from the GCC region. Vendors competed against each other for customers by offering free samples of dates, of various colors, sizes, textures, and quality. While checking out the bounty, Monica could readily recognize some of them: the soft and black ones were Anbarah dates, the yellow and crunchy ones were Barhi, and the large, brown ones were Safawi. Naturally, the higher the grade of the dates, the costlier they were. Monica's eyes bulged when she saw the price per kilogram of the Anbarah dates: 400 riyals, which was equivalent to $108 USD. *Mercy!* she thought to herself. That was too steep for her taste buds. Therefore, she gravitated towards the stalls that displayed the more budget-friendly dates.

While in the process of narrowing down her choices, Monica heard a man's angry voice behind her shouting in Arabic. Curious, she turned around and saw two stern looking men with full beards watching her. She immediately recognized them as members of the Commission for the Promotion of Virtue and Prevention of Vice – aka the Mutawah, the religious/morality police. Their job was to enforce Sharia laws on social conduct in the Kingdom. They were directly employed by the King and had the power to detain and arrest residents, plus shut down businesses. The Mutawah ensured that there was no impropriety occurring between the sexes. Additionally, they closely monitored women's appearance to eliminate the risk of them appearing other than chaste in public. As such, females were expected to wear a black abaya and niqab once they departed their residence.

This religious order caught the world's attention in the early 2000s due to a controversial and tragic event. Fifteen Saudi schoolgirls had perished in a fire that had broken out in their school. In their confusion, they couldn't find their headscarves and abayas. Therefore, the Mutawah at the scene refused to let them exit the building.

Keeping this incident in mind, Monica was fully prepared to cooperate with the two menacing men. Since she was properly dressed, she was curious as to why they had accosted her. The taller and bigger man folded his arms across his broad chest and aggressively stood a few inches from her face. Like most Americans, Monica was big on personal space; therefore, she took a few steps back from her aggressor. Silence fell on the area, as both sellers and potential buyers tuned in to watch the drama unfold.

"Are you African?" he asked loudly.

"No, Amrike. What's the problem?"

"Are you Muslim?" he probed.

Not liking his tone of voice and aggressiveness, Monica replied with an attitude. "No, I'm not. What's. The. Problem?"

He glanced briefly at his partner, then returned his gaze to Monica. Next, he took another step toward her. He was so close to her, their faces almost touched. Monica's jaw dropped when his voice boomed, "You're a man in an abaya. Take off the niqab!" She couldn't believe her ears. WTF! Because she was very tall, willowy and wore her hair short, she was a man? Knowing the power that the Mutawah wielded in the Kingdom, Monica resentfully complied with the man's order. As she pulled the niqab off her face, she seethed and said, "I'm NOT a man! I'm a woman." For good measure, she also took her iqama out of her handbag and showed it to her antagonists. Both men studied Monica's face and resident card intently for what seemed an eternity. Then they glanced at each other, lowered their heads in apology and backed away from her. Monica glared at them briefly before she replaced her niqab. As she walked past the two goons, she muttered a few expletives under her breath.

Monica was disgusted and had lost all interest in the dates and festival. With as much grace and dignity that she could muster, she stretched her limbs to her full six-foot frame and walked haughtily towards the entrance of the venue. There were a few taxis parked on the sidewalk by the festival grounds. Monica made her way to the first one. "The Movenpick hotel, please," she instructed the taxi driver as she opened the rear door. She still bristled at the memory of her recent encounter with the Mutawah and was in no mood to converse with the cabbie. However, he was oblivious to her feelings and proceeded to engage her in conversation.

"So, where are you from?" he inquired casually.

"The USA," Monica replied stiffly, then looked out the window. He didn't take the hint and continued, "Oh, America! I've always wanted to visit." Not wanting to appear the "ugly American" Monica forced herself to be cordial. "And you?" she asked.

"I'm from Kerala," the man stated proudly.

"That's nice. I've heard that there are many beautiful beaches there."

"Yes, that's true. You must visit there someday."

The driver told Monica that his name was Nazir and he had been living in Al Qassim for nineteen years. "That's a long time, you must really like it here," she remarked in genuine amazement. "I do, but things are heating up around here and I no longer feel safe. I think that it's time for me to go back to my country." Monica's interest was mildly piqued, "Oh?" she replied.

Nazir proceeded to tell her about the sixty Al Qaeda members who were arrested nearby his home earlier this year; and, about the two men he recently picked up late one night who requested to be taken to the hospital. "As I was loading their bags into the trunk of the taxi, I realized that they contained guns. So, I dropped the men off near their destination. I told them that I wasn't sure of the exact location of the hospital and not to bother to pay me their fare." Nazir's revelations scared Monica. She admired his courage in continuing to live in Al Qassim. Premium dates or not, Monica couldn't wait to leave this rinky-dink town the next morning.

CHAPTER

20

WHEN PAMELA FIRST ARRIVED IN Saudi Arabia - ambitious and vibrant - she had craved the lifestyle of the well-heeled expat housewives whom she had admired and envied from a distance. A decade later, her wish had come true and she was now an honorable member of that very club. All things considered, Pamela had become the woman she wanted to be. The shopping sprees, exotic vacations, and parties, had all been marvelous. However, they had come at great expense – both personally and professionally. They had come at a price that Pamela hadn't initially bargained on paying, and honestly, did not feel was worthwhile continuing to pay. In addition to the strain on her marriage, her loss of independence, and career opportunities, were also beginning to take their toll on her both mentally and emotionally.

From personal knowledge, she knew all too well the risks of living in the fast lane indefinitely. She had witnessed the demise of several acquaintances whose lifestyle of excess had resulted in them succumbing to adultery, depression, and/or painkillers. The last one to bite the dust had a nervous breakdown. As far as Pamela was concerned, no amount of material success was worth any of these side effects. Although she prided herself in being grounded, she knew that the potential was still there for her to self-destruct. Saudi Arabia just seemed to have a negative effect on expats who lingered too long. Indeed, the pain now outweighed the gain for Pamela. Therefore, the time had come for her to cut her losses and move on.

She had approximately one hour before Glenn's expected return home. So, she went online and finished planning her travel itinerary. Pamela had made a killing from the sale of her beautiful outfits and had enough cash to keep her comfortably afloat for at least six months. She had always wanted to visit New Orleans, New York, Boston and Las Vegas. And so, she googled travelers' reviews of accommodations and sights in these cities. After booking several hotel rooms, Pamela - on a whim - decided to do a job search in those areas.

Having left her quiet hometown so long ago, she felt that she had outgrown it. Apart from visiting her parents, there really wasn't any strong desire on her part to resettle there. Over the years, friendships had become labored and superficial. And of course, Pamela herself had changed. To start anew, it was necessary for her to rebuild her life in another place. Pamela saw several appealing entry-level ads for engineers at companies in Boston and New York. She could see herself doing well in either city. Carefully, she jotted down the point of contact details, and placed the slip of paper in her day planner. When she arrives in those cities, she will touch base with these people. Who knows, perhaps, she will get lucky and land a job at one of these firms.

CHAPTER

21

ONE WEEK AFTER RAMADHAN ENDED, Khalid and I were officially joined in matrimony. Keeping with the Saudi marital tradition, Khalid had to get permission to marry me since I am a foreigner. As soon as he received consent, we went with his father and the Imam - from the mosque where they are congregants - to the court. The judge read several passages from the Holy Qur'an, then inquired if I agreed to marry Khalid, to which I enthusiastically replied, "YES." Next, we signed our wedding contract stipulating the terms of our union, and some papers required for obtaining our marriage license from the Interior Ministry.

According to Islamic law, the bride's father must be present at her ceremony. However, in a case like mine where the woman's father isn't Muslim, this rule does not apply. Converted Muslim women - such as yours truly - must have a Muslim guardian (Wali) or Imam from the community represent her in court. This is the reason why the Imam from Khalid's mosque accompanied us to the court. Once all the documents were signed, I felt a huge wave of relief wash over me. Now that Khalid and I were officially married, we wouldn't have to hide our relationship and sneak around anymore.

As my wedding day drew closer and closer, I became a nervous wreck. Although I was readily embraced by Khalid's immediate family, I also wanted to pass muster with his entire tribe, and friends. Well, on second thought, I wanted to do more than just pass muster; I wanted to "Wow" them. Never mind the fact that my interactions with his loved ones would be limited, I still felt somewhat pressured

74

to make a great first impression on them. Now, before you go laying blame at my beloved's feet, I must let you know that he at no time pressured me. It was only my immense love for him that was driving me to put my best foot forward at our wedding.

Some of you are probably thinking that I was being foolish to push myself so hard, to gain the admiration and respect of a bunch of strangers. I hear you, but since these people matter a great deal to Khalid, and he matters a whole lot to me, by extension they are relevant to me too. So, while I really shouldn't care whether they embrace me or not, the bottom line is that I do. Although I've never discussed with Khalid how much emphasis he placed on his relatives' and friends' assessment of me, I'm positive that he valued their opinions a whole lot. Therefore, even if he only saw his assortment of uncles, aunts, cousins, and buddies several times a year, there's no doubt in my mind that their opinions about his choice of a wife - and a foreign one at that - mattered hugely to him.

Since I knew how important our wedding would be to Khalid and his parents, and I didn't want to let them down, I meekly went along with their plans for our big event. For starters, there were several appointments with the dermatologist to rid me of my dreadful under eye dark circles. There were also trips to the dentist to whiten my coffee-stained teeth. Likewise, spa treatments and consultations with cosmetologists, hair stylists and photographers.

I'm really fortunate that Mrs. Abeer and I share the same taste in fashion; therefore, we were on the same page about the type of wedding gown that I wanted to wear. After pouring over many photos of western-style wedding gowns by fashion mavens such as Vera Wang and Elie Saab, she and I settled on a modest silk faille A-line gown adorned with hand-cut lace. As more fittings with the seamstress, Mrs. Hamida, followed and I saw the beautiful garment materialize, the reality of my upcoming nuptials hit me hard. So, one afternoon, while Mrs. Hamida was pinning my wedding gown bustle, I suddenly burst into tears. "Tut, habibte," she said and smiled, "You're going to be fine." I desperately wanted to believe her, but I wasn't 100 percent convinced that I would indeed be fine. While I was gaining a husband and a new family, the status of my old family – by that I mean my parents, was uncertain. Would they eventually come to terms with my marriage and welcome me and my new family into the fold? Or would they and I end up severing ties completely? Would Khalid's extended family approve of me? More importantly, would Khalid and I be truly happy together for the rest of our lives? While I pondered these troubling thoughts, a pin prick interrupted my brooding and brought me back to the present. "Ouch!" I cried out when I felt a slight tingling sensation in my butt. "Mrs. Hamida, please be careful."

Although Mrs. Abeer and I saw eye to eye on most of the wedding plans, we had a disconnect regarding the venue for the wedding. Perhaps it would be more accurate to say that Dr. Mahmood and I were the ones with the disconnect. The thought of Khalid and I being forced to have separate wedding celebrations in Saudi Arabia was very hard for me to accept. So, one morning when Mrs. Abeer and I were reviewing her wedding guest list, I boldly suggested to her that instead of Jeddah - as initially planned - Khalid and I should have our wedding in either Manama or Dubai. This way, we would be able to celebrate our special day together. Since it is Saudi custom for the groom's family to pay all related expenses associated with the wedding, I dared not demand that Dr. Mahmood and Mrs. Abeer honor my request. I just hoped and prayed that they would grant my very reasonable wish. I'm pleased to report that Mrs. Abeer was quite empathetic and receptive to my idea; and she promised to discuss the matter with her husband. Later that evening, Mrs. Abeer informed me that Dr. Mahmood felt that switching venues from domestic to overseas would be too complicated because the ballroom in Jeddah had already been booked. However, he would be happy to fund Khalid's and my honeymoon abroad.

And so, I unenthusiastically accepted their compromise. Dreaming often about our honeymoon helped to take my mind off the disappointment about our wedding venue. This might sound odd to you, although I wanted to have my wedding celebration in Dubai or Manama, I didn't want to honeymoon in either location. While cosmopolitan, these two cities are just too busy and overly developed for my taste. When I think of a honeymoon destination, Salalah in Oman immediately comes to mind. It is utterly breathtakingly beautiful and rustic! The coconut plantations, pristine beaches, and seclusion, all make it the perfect place for a romantic honeymoon. So, later that night, I discussed with my beloved the prospect of us honeymooning in Salalah.

CHAPTER
22

Y ASMIN SPILLED THE CUP OF coffee she was drinking on her favorite cream-color kurta when she read the crude message in her inbox. It was anonymously sent to Vicki and cc'd to all staff: "You Fat Fu*k!" went the opening line. Yasmin's mouth opened and closed in disbelief as she read the vile message. *What kind of females am I working with?* she asked herself. From the construction of the email, Yasmin was positive that several people were involved in the dirty deed. Some paragraphs were written amateurishly, while others were quite florid. Regardless, the message was malicious and unprofessional. *How cowardly!* Yasmin thought to herself as she grabbed her books and went to class.

Things were certainly falling apart. The work environment had grown so toxic in the six months that Yasmin had been employed at the college that she now dreaded the work week. Every workday when her alarm clock sounded, Yasmin developed a curious pain at the nape of her neck and across her shoulders. It took every ounce of her willpower to roll out of bed in the mornings. "It's all the stress from the job," Lydia stated matter-of-factly to Yasmin one evening as they sat in their usual spots by the swimming pool. "You see all those women standing over there?" Lydia gestured with a raising and lowering of her head, "None of them smoked when they first arrived. Now, look at them puffing away like chimneys." Yasmin looked at the group of women – a total of five. She certainly didn't want to end up like them because of this job. She would rather quit her miserable position than start smoking nicotine. Besides, in Islam, cigarette smoking was haram.

Two things that Yasmin admired about Lydia were her cool and her sense of style. Although Yasmin felt at times Lydia was a bit too cool. Her facial expression never betrayed her emotions. She was always sangfroid as the French would say; and this resulted in some of their colleagues erroneously labeling Lydia as aloof. While a few teachers occasionally looked nice, Lydia always looked good. Her make-up was applied with care, hair well-coiffed, fingers perfectly manicured, and clothes conservative, but stylish.

"What's your secret?" Yasmin shyly asked Lydia one afternoon.

Lydia turned to face Yasmin and responded guardedly, "To what?"

"Your secret to being so calm," Yasmin clarified.

Lydia's mouth creased into a slow smile. "Oh, yoga and meditation," she replied.

Before Yasmin could get a chance to ask Lydia about the type of yoga she practiced, Lydia closed her eyes and put her headphones on her head.

Yasmin was having a hard time concentrating on the lesson. Thoughts about the culprits behind the cruel email to Vicki kept invading her mind. So, she decided to preoccupy her students with a writing assignment, relieving herself of the duty of active teaching. While her students attempted the task, Yasmin mentally evaluated each of her peers to guess the identity of the guilty ones. Who on staff was tech savvy enough to send such an email anonymously? Who has had open conflict with Vicki? Who stood to gain from this mess if Vicki was to resign? As Yasmin pondered these questions, the bell rang, and jolted her from her contemplation. She was relieved that the school day was over and looked forward to hanging out with Lydia. As her students quickly flung on their abayas and dashed out the classroom door, Yasmin called after them, "Banats, please finish your paragraphs for homework!"

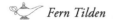

Yasmin was one of the first to board the bus that afternoon. She sat in the middle where she could get a good look at her colleagues as they got on the bus. As they entered the vehicle, she scrutinized each of them. Hmph, nobody looked guilty, or behaved out of the ordinary. It was business as usual. The only tell-tale sign that something was amiss was Vicki's absence. No closer to solving this mystery, Yasmin sighed and whipped out her Kindle. *Some people have no morals, but Allah knows what's in every heart,* she thought to herself as she picked up where she had left off in Dale Carnegie's book, *How to Enjoy Your Life and Your Job.*

Yasmin had never been big on physical fitness. Like most females, she only exercised when she wanted to lose some kilos for some special event. She didn't care for gyms as she was self-conscious about her appearance. As far as she could see, the only people who worked out at the gym were those who were already in shape. So, she wasn't going to embarrass herself in front of those fitness fiends. Yasmin had always heard that jogging and running were the fastest ways to burn calories and lose weight. While neither of these activities appealed to her, she did however, enjoy walking. So, one day when Fitness Superstore was having a sale, Yasmin invested in a treadmill. It was a good thing that she bought it on sale because she rarely used it. Once in a blue moon she would get on her treadmill for half an hour, but most of the time, she just dusted it off when she cleaned her bedroom.

Since relocating to the Kingdom, Yasmin had gained several kilos. A result of eating all the rich Saudi food and not exercising. She noticed that many Saudis were obese and had heard that diabetes was the main health issue in the Kingdom. That should have been motivation enough for her to change her eating habits and get back into shape, but it wasn't. After all the drama earlier on, Yasmin felt like blowing off some steam. Initially, she was going to ask Lydia if she could join her for meditation and yoga, but changed her mind. Lydia was a loner, and most likely wouldn't want company. Besides, some yoga poses, and chants, were haram. Therefore, Yasmin decided instead, to walk the perimeter of the compound for forty minutes. There was a lovely breeze blowing, so she was enjoying her walk. As she strode briskly around the area, she admired the beautiful landscaping and the local amenities. The gym, swimming pools, tennis court, and playground were all maintained at very high standards by the Indian laborers. She had never really taken notice before of how lovely the compound grounds and facilities really were because her usual routine was to lounge by the swimming pool. Now that she knew, and the weather was getting cooler, she would mix things up a bit.

When Yasmin turned the corner where the management team resided, she spotted Vicki. "You alright?" Yasmin inquired sympathetically. Her supervisor's eyes were red and swollen from crying. Although Vicki didn't believe in fraternizing with her subordinates, she needed to talk to somebody. Feeling that she could trust Yasmin, she replied truthfully, "No, I'm not. Do you have a minute?" Yasmin looked around quickly before she slipped into her manager's flat. As Vicki in between tears told Yasmin about all the dodginess that was going on behind the scenes with the dean, Yasmin's head began to throb, and she felt nauseous. She squinted at her superior in disbelief. There was no doubt in her mind that all the sordid details she was being made privy to were true. The dean had always struck Yasmin as a calculating and ruthless woman. And so, she had been careful not to cross her path. Her luck was about to run out though, when she bumped into the dean after leaving Vicki's flat. Yasmin gave her a weak smile and half-hearted greeting. *Crap! This isn't good,* she panicked. As Yasmin continued her walk around the perimeter, she wondered what repercussions she would face. *Why, oh why did I agree to lend a sympathetic ear?* she scolded herself. Somethings would have been better left unsaid and unknown.

CHAPTER

23

ONE MONDAY MORNING, SHORTLY AFTER four o'clock, Monica's slumber was disturbed by a loud crashing sound. Yawning loudly, she sat up in bed and rubbed her eyes. The din of glass breaking and furniture toppling over, forced her to jump out of bed. *What the dickens is going on?* she wondered. The commotion was coming from across the hallway from Anna's apartment. Silently, Monica tip-toed to her front door. She was about to ease it open when she heard the clatter of many footsteps and a male's voice. She recognized the speaker to be the director, Edgar. He pounded his fist on Anna's door, and commanded her to open it. A woman's voice shrieked back at him, "Fu*k off!"

Monica heard several doors in the hallway open and some murmurs. Gently, she eased her door open a crack and peeped outside. She saw Edgar, the compound manager, Carl, and three policemen standing in front of Anna's door. Edgar was speaking rapidly into his cellphone. "Hurry-up!" he barked, then disconnected the call. Soon, there was a strong smell of ketchup and some liquid - black in color - hissed and seeped from under Anna's door into the corridor. "What the ---?!" Edgar said as the substance headed towards his white slide-slippers. The policemen looked at the liquid rapidly blanketing the floor and stepped back from the door.

A few minutes later, Susan came panting into view. Three pink foam curlers protruded from the front of her colorful bonnet. And her abaya - which was partially open - revealed her Miss Piggy pajama set. Despite the seriousness of the situation, Monica felt the corners of her mouth twitch and she stifled the urge to laugh. Susan hurriedly joined Edgar. "Sorry for the delay," she wheezed. "I was trying to locate Anna's mobile number on our staff telephone directory." Frantically, she dialed Anna's number. The sound of her phone ringing competed against the din of glass crashing to the floor. Shortly thereafter, there was a thud and the ringing stopped. "That didn't go very well," Susan said, to no one in particular.

Edgar turned to Carl and instructed him to open Anna's door. The manager fumbled with a ring of keys before he located the correct key. Gingerly, he turned the handle of the door and stepped aside. Anna's mangled cellphone was the first thing they saw on the floor. "Anna," Susan said in a soft and gentle tone of voice, "we're coming in." Cautiously, the police entered Anna's apartment. After several minutes, the senior police officer raised his hand, and signaled for Edgar and Susan to join them. Carefully, they stepped over the broken glass and objects strewn all over the floor. Susan gasped when she saw Anna. She was scribbling obscene messages on the living room wall with a blue magic marker. Susan's face turned beet red when she read the unflattering words Anna had written specifically about her. *Hmph! So, this is how she truly feels about me. After all that I did to make her feel welcome.* Susan thought to herself. Anna was oblivious to their presence and appeared to be in a state of deep concentration as she expressed her thoughts on the wall about several of her colleagues. Edgar and Susan exchanged a glance. Susan tried to keep the anger out of her voice when she eventually spoke. "Anna!" she called again from a safe distance. Anna dropped her marker, stood back and admired her handiwork. Next, she looked at her walls splattered with ketchup. Lastly, she surveyed her floor littered with broken glass, crockery, and toppled furniture. "Anna!" Susan shouted this time. With a jolt, Anna looked at them. Edgar proceeded to walk towards her, but stopped in his tracks when she started to yell, "Rape, Rape!" and threw a can of Diet Coke at him.

As soon as the bus dropped the teachers off at the university, Susan called an emergency staff meeting. "As many of you probably already know," she began, "there was an unfortunate incident involving one of our colleagues earlier this morning. Anna is currently getting the necessary medical attention that she needs. In the meantime, I'll be splitting up her classes among several of you. Six of you will each get four of her students added to your sections. Thanks so much for your continued hard work… stay strong."

After the meeting, Lauren and Monica quickly walked back to their office and closed the door. In unison, they raised their eyebrows, sighed, and shook their heads. "What have we gotten ourselves into, Monica?"

"Only the good Lord knows, my friend."

"Do you think that this place got to Anna, or she was already cuckoo?"

"Well, I overheard Susan telling one of the coordinators that Anna had been taking medication for some mental disorder, but her prescription had run out."

"Oh dear! Thank God she flipped on the compound. Can you imagine if she'd gone berserk in her classroom?"

"Girlfriend, I don't even want to THINK about that!"

"I think that the Saudi government, when reviewing applications for work visas, should also investigate the applicants' mental health – not just screen for STDs and drug use."

"I'm totally with you. All of us are put at risk when exposed to people like Anna. Her behavior this morning really freaked me out. I noticed that she was very moody, but I had no idea that there was a lot more to her mood swings."

After a brief silence, Monica spoke. "This may be a terrible thing to say, and I probably shouldn't ask you this, but do you think that Anna is truly cuckoo? Or do you believe that she's just pretending to be mad, so she can get out of this crappy contract?"

"You know, it's funny that you should ask. I was wondering the same thing," confessed Lauren.

84

"Now, this is strictly between us," Lauren continued.

"But of course," Monica replied. "Cross my heart."

"Well, according to the grapevine, when Anna trashed her apartment, she primarily damaged the institution's property. The few personal items of hers that she did destroy were of little monetary value."

"Oh?" Monica replied, her interest aroused.

"AND…" Lauren continued, ignoring Monica's interruption, "several U.S. one-dollar bills were found partially burnt in Anna's kitchen sink, but none of the fives, tens, or twenties, which lay scattered over her kitchen counter."

"Ahh, the plot thickens. So, Sherlock, what do you deduce?" Monica prodded.

Grinning, Lauren replied, "My dear Watson, the evidence would indicate that Anna is playing us for fools! Anyhow, jokes aside, her actions corroborate the claims of some psychologists that there's no such thing as insanity."

"No kidding! Well, even if she was pulling our legs, I do believe that she's crying out for help," Monica replied. "Her behavior is not normal."

The bell rang, indicating the start of the first class for the day and simultaneously the end of their conversation.

CHAPTER
24

I F YOU CAN IMAGINE A girls' night out on the town, fashion show, and New Year's Eve party all rolled into one, you'll have a pretty good idea of my wedding function (and what a typical Saudi wedding event is like). The female guests arrived decked out in their finest jewelry and gowns. Some single ladies, on the market for a husband, drew attention to themselves by dancing up a storm in hopes of catching the eye of a potential future mother-in-law. My party was in full swing after I made my debut at midnight. Since Khalid's family is very liberal, you'll be pleased to know that a belly dancer, a singer, and a trio of Sudanese drummers performed at my function. And there was a good amount of merrymaking that night.

I suppose I should be grateful that it's the custom for the Saudi bride to get all dolled up only to sit alone in her dressing room for most of her wedding event. This spared me having to endure my guests' scrutiny for any long period of time. My guests - all female relatives and close friends of Khalid's and his parents' - started arriving around nine, and the party got underway shortly after eleven. From all the laughter and chatter, I assumed everybody was having a great time.

At midnight, I made my brief, but grand entrance. You can well imagine my nervousness! The spotlight was literally on me the minute I stepped out of my dressing room and remained my constant companion all the way to the stage. For support, I lightly gripped the bannister - which was elegantly swathed in white chiffon fabric - as I made my way slowly down the long flight of stairs. While gliding past the guests, I tried not to think about the hundreds of probing, unfamiliar eyes - in the packed ballroom - that were now focused on me. Silently, I prayed that I wouldn't trip on my exquisite hem. Oh, how I wished that Khalid could have been by my side for this never-ending walk down this plush aisle strewn with rose petals. Thinking of my beloved made me feel better and somewhat settled the butterflies in my belly. As I continued along my journey to the dais, step by agonizing step, I heard several "oohs" and "aahs" which further strengthened me. When I was almost at the stage, my eyes locked with Mrs. Abeer's and I knew that I was going to be alright. Pride and joy radiated from her pores as she clapped her hands and smiled at me. After several praises were given to the Prophet (PBUH), it was time to pose for photos. Before I knew it, my twenty minutes of fame were over, and I eagerly retreated to my dressing room, leaving my guests to the feast and festivities. Back in my dressing room, I took several selfies and sent them to Khalid with the text message: Wishing you were here. Can't wait for us to be together. MUAH!

Even though my parents and I were estranged, and they didn't really miss much in terms of my wedding, I still regretted that they weren't here to share this moment. Granted, my dad would have had to attend Khalid's ceremony instead of mine. Nevertheless, he would still be partaking in a very important piece of my life as he would get to know his son-in-law and Dr. Mahmood better. While I have the utmost respect for my mother-in-law, who I now call "Mother Abeer," and am truly appreciative of all that she has done for me, I can't help but think how wonderful it would have been for my birth mother to have been involved in my wedding preparations too. Especially since I never planned to get married, and my mother wasn't expecting me to do so. But it is what it is. For what it's worth, as soon as the wedding photos are ready, I'm going to send them to my parents.

CHAPTER
25

Y ASMIN ISN'T THE TYPE OF person to air dirty linen in public. So, it hurt her to admit the following, but after going on pilgrimage, she had to concede that Saudi Muslims and expat Muslims aren't really "one." While all Muslims might be "one" in Allah's eyes, the Muslim expats in the Kingdom clearly aren't viewed in the same light by their Saudi brethren and sisters. Sometimes, Yasmin wondered if they were all serving the same God. How could the Saudis in good conscience treat other Muslims so shabbily? Especially on a pilgrimage to do Hajj and Umrah. Despite already knowing that people like her aren't really accepted, or thought highly of in Saudi Arabia - and the Gulf region for that matter - Yasmin was still stunned when she traveled to Makkah for Umrah and experienced first-hand subtle racism. Several weeks later, she was still trying to come to terms with her feelings of alienation and discrimination while on pilgrimage. Umrah is the optional pilgrimage Muslims take at any time of the year outside of the mandatory pilgrimage dates for Hajj. The purpose of Umrah is for Muslims to cleanse their souls of past sins.

While gender segregation in mosques is a way of life in Saudi Arabia, Yasmin was surprised by the additional separation by nationality for pilgrims. In all her readings of the Holy Qur'an, there was no verse in it that mentioned Muslims on pilgrimage must be partitioned according to their homeland. Of course, since her physical features screamed "Indian/Pakistani," Yasmin was ordered to sit with the Indian and Pakistani female pilgrims instead of her fellow British nationals. Although Yasmin was quite proud of her heritage and would never dream of denying her roots, she was disturbed by this rule which only served to create additional barriers between Muslim people. As far as she was concerned, Muslims were already very much divided by country of origin, skin color, language, and social class. This additional separation on pilgrimage didn't help matters.

Apart from this issue, Yasmin's spiritual journey itself was incredible. She was humbled to have been able to perform Umrah at the Haram Sharif. It was quite an experience for her to witness the Ka'bah with her own two eyes; and later, to recite the Holy verses and do supplications in that highly-charged space. It was true what people said about there being strength in numbers. Yasmin could feel how powerful their collective rakaats were at that sacred site. Drinking the Holy water at the Zamzam Well refreshed and nourished her. She even collected four bottles of that precious water to take home to her family. At the completion of Umrah, Yasmin felt an overwhelming sense of peace and clarity wash over her.

She knew that she was fortunate to be able to afford Umrah. However, she strongly believed that pilgrimage shouldn't be a privilege, but a right for all Muslims. One of the biggest deterrents to her less fortunate Muslim brothers' and sisters' ability to go on pilgrimage was the obscene hotel room rates. This was ironic because the Qur'an cautions against greed; the hoteliers in these holiest of cities appear to have forgotten this important teaching. Since accommodations near the mosque were limited, only pilgrims with the deepest pockets could afford lodging. It was quite shocking and sad for Yasmin to see her less fortunate brothers and sisters resort to sleeping in their cars at nighttime. Although it was very hot in the daytime, it got darn cold at nighttime.

On two occasions when returning to the hotel where she had accommodations, Yasmin noticed a middle-aged couple huddled on a bench nearby. After striking up a conversation with them, she learned that they were pilgrims from Kabul. They told her that they had used up all their savings to make this journey. Feeling compassion for them, the next morning, Yasmin went to the souq - around the corner from the hotel - and purchased a blanket for them. While Sadaqa (voluntary charity) is encouraged in Islam, by nature Yasmin has a social conscience and is civic-minded. As such, she's committed to doing her part to right the wrongs in her culture. Therefore, the next time she called her parents, she told them her idea for starting a local foundation to sponsor needy Pakistani Brits for Hajj and Umrah.

CHAPTER

26

T HE TAXI DROPPED LAUREN AND Monica off in front
of the sprawling Salam Camp at a quarter of five, one sunny
Thursday afternoon. The wide tree-lined streets sprinkled with
stately, stone houses and well-manicured lawns seemed out of place
in the desert. One could easily forget that he/she was in Saudi
Arabia. Salam Camp could have been any suburban community in
the USA.

"Wow, are we really still in Saudi Arabia?" Monica inquired. "I
didn't know that there were areas that are so green."

Lauren chuckled and replied, "Talk about having it made in the
shade. This is what it means to be in the lap of luxury!"

"We need to find us some dates here, girlfriend. I definitely
could get used to this!"

"But, are you willing to pay the price my friend? This segment
of the expat population has the highest divorce rate."

"Oh...Really?"

"Yep. Many of these oil expat wives can't handle life here long-
term and end up leaving their husbands."

"That's sad. Do you think that's the case with this lady?"

Before Lauren could reply, she spied Pamela walking towards
them. She waved, and they waved back. Pamela greeted them
warmly, then signed them in at the security office. As the pals
trailed behind Pamela, they quietly absorbed the opulence of her
insulated community. They passed by horseback riding trails, and
squash and tennis courts. They also walked by neat signs directing

residents to various places such as: the bowling alley, golf course, hypermarket, salon, and theatre. A few minutes into their walk, a middle-aged couple wearing matching polo shirts and khaki chinos stopped to chat with Pamela. While they told her about their latest round of golf, Lauren silently admired their set of PXG clubs in the back of their golf cart. Her brother, Richard, would have given his front teeth for them.

From Pamela's speech, Lauren gathered that she was in the company of a fellow Southerner. So, after Pamela's neighbors drove away, she said to her, "I take it that you are originally from the south?"

"Why, yes I am."

"Me, too. I'm from Kentucky"

"Is that right? I'm from Terrell Hills, Texas."

Monica smiled as she listened to Pamela and Lauren's dialogue. She was positive that they didn't realize how Southern they sounded.

Monica and Lauren exchanged a glance when they entered Pamela's splendid villa. It was tastefully furnished with an eclectic mix of floral chintzes, batiks, African sculptures, brass-and-crystal chandeliers, polished wood, jute rugs, and artwork by renowned Arab artists. Although sophisticated, Pamela's well-appointed living room was not intimidating. Guests would feel comfortable putting their feet up on her blue and ivory striped cotton ottomans. "So, these are the things that I have for sale," Pamela gestured with her right hand. Lauren immediately gravitated towards the Vitamix. "Ooh, I've always wanted one of these...how much are you asking for it?" she inquired hesitantly. Pamela looked at her and replied, "Pay me what you like. I've used it regularly for the past seven years." They settled on 1,500 SAR.

While Lauren and Pamela talked about the Vitamix, Monica took the opportunity to admire Pamela's home furnishings in-depth. Her eyes roved appreciatively over the wicker furniture, the leather-bound books, the graceful hurricane lamps and candlesticks, the hand-woven baskets, the home accents in brass, crystal, porcelain, and silver. She admired the unstudied charm and patina of the objects that gave the room its homey ambience. First, she ran her fingers lightly over a peach-pink peony and hummingbird needlepoint covered armchair, enjoying the luxurious feel of the natural linen fabric. Next, she studied the oval, sunburst mirror hanging over the richly textured cream-gold damask sofa. She was positive that the mirror was an antique. The mirror was flanked by two large charcoal drawings of a camel caravan in the Sahara Desert. *Very, very nice,* Monica thought to herself as her eyes swept around the room. She really liked Pamela's style. Understated, yet glamorous, in a nonchalant kind of way.

She felt a twinge of envy when her keen eye spied Pamela's superb collection of blue-and-white Chinese ginger jars displayed in a stylish curio cabinet. Monica had first been exposed to oriental artwork as a college sophomore. While browsing the interior design books at her campus library one afternoon, she had seen a fascinating book on East Asian decorative art and design in the seventeenth and eighteenth centuries. The images in that book cemented her love of chinoiserie and japonaiserie. And so, she promised herself that when her ship came in, she would start collecting antique Chinese and Japanese porcelain. As Monica mulled over whether Pamela's Imari jars were originals or reproductions, Lauren's voice intruded on her thoughts. "Are you buying anything Monica?" she asked. Monica quickly scanned the sale items. She was tempted to buy Pamela's travel guides. She picked up the one on Jordan and flipped through it. Pamela read Monica's mind and decided to sweeten the deal. "If you want to purchase the travel guides, I'll throw in my Conde Nast mags for free." Monica, being a sucker for a bargain, chuckled and replied, "Sold." Feeling generous, Pamela then told her guests to help themselves to any of the other sale items that caught their fancy. So, Lauren grabbed a set of six hand-painted juice glasses. "How about you Monica?" Pamela coaxed. "No, thanks. I'm good," she replied.

Business out the way, Pamela invited her guests to sit in the living room and offered each of them a glass of homemade iced tea. She was curious about their experiences teaching in the Kingdom;

therefore, they humored her with outrageous classroom tales. Pamela hooted with laughter and shook her head in amazement.

"Stop lying! Did a student <u>really</u> use a cigarette lighter to set another girl's hair on fire?"

"Yes, ma'am. She sure did!" replied Lauren. "I tell you only true stories."

"This is the reason why we must keep the Sunni and Shia students separate from each other," Monica chimed in. "They don't play."

"The guys have it worse though," Lauren confided.

"That's right," Monica agreed. "Not too long ago, a male colleague received a video of a man being beheaded and the simple message, 'You're next.' The email was sent via a VPN, so the police couldn't track the sender. However, our colleague strongly suspected several of his students."

"Oh my, I don't envy you your jobs," Pamela sputtered and shook her head. She genuinely liked Lauren and Monica. They were real and would have been fun to hang out with occasionally. It was too bad that their paths crossed so late and under such sad circumstances. Half an hour later, Pamela rose from her rattan chair. "Let me give y'all a ride to the front gate," she offered. "You drive?" Monica asked in amazement. "Now and again I go for a spin around the block, so I don't forget how to drive. One beautiful thing about living at Salam Camp is that what happens here, stays here," Pamela replied with a wink. As Monica and Lauren exited Pamela's vehicle, she extended her hand, and said, "It was an absolute pleasure meeting you two ladies." Both shook her hand warmly and thanked her for the hospitality.

After loading their purchases in the trunk of a taxi, they waved goodbye to Pamela. "Well, Lauren, what do you think is her story? Just decluttering?" Monica asked. Lauren stared back at the fabulous camp that was now a dot on the horizon and replied, "I dunno, Monica. Your guess is as good as mine."

CHAPTER
27

LIKE MOST COUPLES, KHALID AND I also have hurdles to overcome. One of the biggest for me is the strong influence of his blood relatives on our lives. It took me quite some time to get used to the fact that their needs came before mine. Since I am Khalid's wife, I expected to be his top priority. However, this was hardly the case. If his parents wanted something, Khalid immediately put everything else on hold to accommodate them.

It really ticked me off one Friday evening, when we had to cancel our plans to go furniture shopping at Danube Home. The store was having the sale of all sales on bedroom furniture, that Friday only. And so, I had my heart set on purchasing a mahogany, king-sized four poster bed for our guest room. Well, as luck would have it, Dr. Mahmood was unable to drive Mother Abeer to her weekly Friday visit with her big sister, Heba, who lived on the other side of Riyadh, because he was going out of town. Therefore, my beloved had to do the honors. Well, by the time he returned home from driving his mother across Riyadh, we had less than half an hour remaining to get to Danube Home before it closed. So, we ended up missing this much anticipated sale. To say that I was an unhappy camper would be a gross understatement. I had previously mentioned to Mother Abeer how much I was looking forward to this sale; so, I was disappointed that she wasn't considerate enough to curtail her visit with her sister, or better yet, postpone her trip till the next day. It wasn't as if aunt Heba was sick, or about to take a trip overseas. However, I held my tongue and kept the peace.

While I appreciated the fact that Khalid had a close relationship with his parents, I must confess that I didn't really understand why he was always going over to their house as soon as he got home from work. He may as well have just continued to live with them. Initially, when we bought our house a few doors away from his parents' residence, I thought it would be rather cool to live in such close proximity to them. However, now that we were practically neighbors, and Khalid spent most of his free time with his parents, I began to feel that there was too much family togetherness.

His need to always apprise them of whatever went on behind our closed doors also perplexed me. I wondered, did Khalid also keep his parents abreast of all the minutiae in his life while he lived in London? As far as I'm concerned, we are all adults. So, there's really no reason why Mother Abeer and Dr. Mahmood should know - for example - that I enjoyed smoking shisha on our balcony after dinner. Or, that I preferred to burn incense sticks instead of bakhoor. Or, that I wanted to re-paint our bedroom walls a subtle shade of ivory. I suppose, it wouldn't rankle me so much if my in-laws were kept in the loop, but were gracious enough to keep their silence. However, when Mother Abeer always felt the need to give unsolicited advice, I resented it.

A very awkward moment for me was when Mother Abeer - for a housewarming present - gifted us with a vivid oil painting she had made of her husband assisting Khalid (as a teenager) to mount a very spirited white Arabian steed in the desert. Mother Abeer had perfectly captured and portrayed the struggle for control occurring between the men and the beast in her design. I thought that this fabulous artwork would make a great conversation piece and therefore, I hung it in the foyer. Well, Mother Abeer stopped by unexpectedly one day - as she's wont to do on occasion - and inquired about the painting. I proudly showed it to her prominently displayed on the wall for all to view and admire. Without any hesitation, she made it plain that the landscape was to be hung in the male majilis. Umbrage wouldn't have been taken if Mother

Abeer had gently suggested that the male majilis would be a more appropriate location for her artwork. However, I must confess that I was quite offended by her blatantly telling me that the men's majilis was the place she wanted the painting to be hung. This was after all, my domain. And as the queen of my castle, I should have the pleasure of making that decision.

Perhaps, I was to blame for Mother Abeer's taking control of my home and life. After all, I had, up until this point, given her free rein to run the show. For starters, I went along with her program for my wedding. Then, I made no objections to her ideas on the décor of our new home. She instructed that the walls be painted a burnt orange; and stated, that deep plum and coral were a must for tapestries and fringe curtains. Check. Next, she had put me in touch with her interior designer to assist me with ordering floor cushions, bolsters, poufs, and ottomans in sumptuous fabrics. Furthermore, she instructed that three specific Bedouin women in Anak village were to be commissioned to weave our arabesque wool rugs and stair runner. Sorted. Also, she insisted that traditional lanterns and other light fixtures were to be gold-embellished. Done. On top of that, she stressed that mother-of-pearl inlaid Moroccan furniture was essential for completing "the look." Once again, I complied with her wishes. So, I guess I really shouldn't be annoyed that Mother Abeer was now dictating the placement of her painting.

While I've resigned myself to the fact that Khalid's blood relatives are his number one priority, it has still taken me a long time to come to terms with the reality that Islam was in second place for his attention. And so, when he was not socializing with his parents, uncles and cousins, he was communing with Allah, or had fellowship with his brethren at the mosque. If I didn't know better, I would think that he was trying to avoid me. Anyway, I've come to realize that this is the norm for Saudi males; so, I'm working hard not to take Khalid's neglect personally.

I hope that I haven't given you dear readers the impression that I'm a needy woman, who needs her man's validation every step of the way. Let me assure you, I'm no clinging vine. People who know me quite well would describe me as a very independent young woman. I'll be the first to agree that husbands and wives both need personal space in their marriage. However, I believe it is equally as important for couples to spend quality time together for their relationship to blossom. I suppose that under the circumstances, since I married Khalid and into his culture, it's best for me to follow Mother Abeer's lead and just get busy with my life too. Since tying the knot, my blogging and Arabic lessons have been neglected. I think it's time for me to resume these activities.

Some of you might be thinking that my venting is a clear sign of my unhappiness and wondering if I have any regrets about getting married. Absolutely none! While things at times were very frustrating and I often felt like I suffered needlessly, trust me, there's no niggling thought in the back of mind that perhaps I made the wrong decision in marrying Khalid. As you already know, he's a great guy. If he wasn't, I most certainly wouldn't have married him. More importantly, though, he and I have a special connection. He brings out the best in me, and I know we're meant to be soul mates. It's not his fault that he's reverted to acting the way a typical Saudi man does who hasn't been exposed to the western world. And I can totally identify with his powerlessness to behave otherwise in his homeland. He's in a very delicate position of having to conform to societal norms. I, for one, don't envy him. So, while I'll occasionally rant and want to rebel against my new life, believe me, there's no doubt in my mind that my beloved is doing the best that he can for his blood relatives, community, and me. Therefore, if self-sacrificing is required of me, so be it. I'm 100 percent committed to Khalid and our marriage.

CHAPTER
28

N O ONE COULD EVER ACCUSE Monica of being a social butterfly, but she decided to take Yasmin up on her dinner invitation the following month. She probably saw in her something of her former friend, Najah, who is also of Pakistani heritage. While Najah and Yasmin don't physically resemble each other, there's however, something of a spark of insouciance and fierce independence in Yasmin that reminded Monica a lot about Najah. Looking back, Monica would have to say that the best part of her teenage years was meeting Najah. Although she can't pinpoint the exact moment when she and Najah became good friends in high school, she recalled that they were both science majors and had the same biology and physics classes together. Due to Najah's intelligence, she skipped two grades which led to her and Monica's paths crossing.

In high school, Monica thought that she wanted to have a career as a chemical engineer; unfortunately, science didn't come naturally to her. So, she had to work extra hard to get decent grades. Although Monica wouldn't describe herself as an overachiever, by nature she was ambitious. Najah, with her diligence, was the perfect pal for her. She challenged Monica to become a better student. Monica hated it when she didn't score as high a mark as Najah did on tests. She recalled that they had a friendly little competition between them. This motivated Monica to apply herself even more to her lessons, and she strove to beat Najah on exams. "Hah! I scored two points higher than you," Monica remembered saying to Najah good-naturedly on one occasion. With her characteristic grin, Najah replied, "Monica, you got lucky this time, let's see how you do on the next test."

Even though Monica and Najah were from different cultures, they hit it off immediately and would often eat lunch and study together. Although some Americans think that Pakistani-Americans are clannish, Monica was fully embraced by Najah and her family. She never felt like an outsider and spent several wonderful weekends with them at their modest single-family home in Queens, New York. Frankly speaking, this was Monica's first time feeling that she really had a family. Growing up in the South Bronx area of New York City, with only a toxic mother to call family, was very tough for her. And made her eager to turn eighteen, so she could escape her wretched home life.

Understandably, Monica felt relieved when her mother kicked her out of her apartment one weekend. Needing a place to stay, she promptly telephoned Najah and told her about her problem. Despite having many mouths to feed, Najah's parents readily opened their home to Monica. Their generosity of spirit deeply touched her because they weren't rich and didn't care that she wasn't from their culture. So, Monica gratefully accepted their kind offer and went to live with them. Although Monica was an only child, she quickly adjusted to Najah's family, which consisted of her parents, an older sister, and four boisterous younger brothers.

Prior to living with Najah's family, values of discipline, hard work, thrift, and strong familial bonds were novel concepts to Monica. However, she grew to appreciate them while she was a member of Najah's household. Falling into the daily routine of getting up early each morning, eating family meals together, studying for several hours after school, and engaging in conversation instead of watching television, had a positive and lasting impact on Monica. These habits enabled her to survive university and stay grounded. To this day, she continues to get up at the crack of dawn, prioritize her work, and live a frugal life.

As their friendship deepened, Monica seriously thought about converting to Islam; and even began to study literature about the Muslim way of life. Then, after Najah and Monica graduated from high school, their paths diverged. Najah went on to study medicine at an elite, private university in New York; while Monica ended up majoring in English Literature at a State University. They reconnected briefly after completing their degrees before losing touch again. Of course, Monica didn't expect their friendship to last forever, but it still saddened her that she and Najah lost touch with each other after she got married.

Najah was now a successful anesthesiologist, and a proud wife and mother of three adorable children. It had been years since she and Monica had spoken to each other. Sometimes, Monica was tempted to call her. However, when she would pick up the phone to dial Najah's number, she would balk at the sound of the dial tone. Why resurrect the past? Najah had moved on, she must do the same. Regardless, Monica still had fond memories of her time spent living with Najah and her family. Actually, they were some of the best memories of her high school days. There had always been a lot of love, support, and delicious food in Najah's home.

Indeed, Monica was first introduced to samosas and Chicken Karahi at Najah's home. Her mother, Mrs. Sameeha, was an excellent cook. Monica remembered well Mrs. Sameeha's large pots of rice and meat that were always simmering on the stovetop. The intoxicating aroma of onions, spices, and curry, regularly punctuated the air. All these culinary memories caused her to salivate. Having had such an excellent introduction to Pakistani cuisine from Mrs. Sameeha, Monica sincerely hoped that Yasmin was at least a good cook. Although Yasmin didn't request Monica to bring a dish, Monica was going to bring some Kheer for dessert. She hated going to social gatherings empty-handed.

"Wow, your flat's lovely," Monica complimented Yasmin as she gave her a tour of her living quarters. While Monica's compound was nice, Yasmin's was far superior. Everything was modern, new, and inviting. She wouldn't mind having a similar quality of life for a year or two.

So, Monica decided that when she becomes better acquainted with Yasmin, she would make polite inquiries about her workplace and benefits.

Although Yasmin's rooms were furnished in a minimalist style, Monica thought that the interiors still looked chic. She loved the blend of the bright colors and rich textures against the neutral walls. Monica noted carefully the high quality of Yasmin's Spartan belongings. There was a set of four watercolor Mughal miniature paintings on top of the bookcase; three round, embroidered silk cushion covers on the sofa; a sterling silver incense burner on the coffee table, and likewise, a square Persian rug which anchored the living room, all of which bespoke Yasmin's solid, middle-class background.

After the tour, Monica followed her host to the dining table and sat opposite her. When Yasmin served the food, Monica eagerly ate every morsel on her plate. "Mmm, this is so delish!" she squealed in rapture when the succulent meat touched her tongue. Monica closed her eyes in pleasure as she chewed her food. "What's this called?" she asked Yasmin as she took another bite. "Cheers, Monica, I'm glad that you like it. This dish is Malai Seekh Kabab."

"Oh, this is excellent. You're a kitchen goddess!"

Pleased with her guest's compliments, Yasmin beamed and said, "Here, have some more."

Although Monica was stuffed, she didn't refuse her host's generous offer; and gratefully held out her plate for seconds. After Yasmin piled more food on Monica's plate, Monica enthusiastically tucked into her dinner, savoring the rich flavors of the dish. When she had polished off the kababs, she leaned back in her chair and patted her distended belly in contentment. "You can feed me any day of the week, Yasmin." The pals both giggled. "Let me know when you're ready for dessert, Monica. I can't eat all this Kheer by myself." Monica looked at her in mock alarm, and said, "If I eat anymore, I'm going to explode, but I'll do my best to accommodate."

Once she had finished the main course, Monica took a short break from eating to allow her food to digest. When she had made room for dessert, she had a small serving of Kheer. It tasted wonderful! Silently, Monica congratulated herself on her choice of dessert. The Kheer was the perfect accompaniment to Yasmin's delicious meal, and a great way to end her visit. "Thank you so much for the invite, Yasmin. I had a wonderful time," Monica said, with heartfelt appreciation. "Listen, I'm a lousy cook," she continued, "but if you ever fancy going to Rashid Mall for a meal, it would be my pleasure to treat."

CHAPTER

29

PAMELA TRIED NOT TO CRY when Glenn reversed his Audi out of their driveway. Bravely, she waved goodbye to him possibly for the last time. When his car disappeared around the bend in the road, she closed the front door slowly. Leaning against the door, she struggled to regain her composure. *"Pull yourself together, girlfriend,"* Pamela whispered to herself. A few minutes later, she walked into the master bedroom to speak with Ayu who was folding and stacking the bed sheets and towels in the linen closet. She was certainly going to miss her services.

"Mrs. Ayu," she began, "I don't know how I would have managed without you. The place looks immaculate as usual."

"Thank you, madam," Ayu replied, clearly pleased with the compliment.

"Listen, I'm going home for a while and just wanted to thank you for all your wonderful service over the years."

Opening the drawer where she kept jewelry, that she no longer wore, Pamela extracted a lovely 14-kt gold Pandora charms bracelet. Presenting it to her housekeeper, she said, "Mrs. Ayu, I'd like you to have this, please keep it in remembrance of me."

"Oh, bless you, madam," Ayu replied with gratitude.

Ayu, with child-like awe, looked at the twelve pretty charms on her bracelet.

On impulse, Pamela also gifted Ayu three sterling silver necklaces with semi-precious stones; one for each of her three daughters. Ayu was stunned, and thanked Pamela repeatedly for her generous gifts.

"Don't mention it, Mrs. Ayu. You're the best. Take excellent care of yourself and Mr. Glenn for me, please."

As soon as Ayu departed, Pamela started packing her clothes in her Louis Vuitton luggage. Mechanically, she rolled and folded as many of her beloved outfits as she could fit in her suitcases. When she finished packing her bags, she collapsed on Glenn's side of their bed and wept. She wept for her failed marriage; she shed tears because she was scared about being on her own, and because she didn't know what the future had in store for her. All this crying was cathartic; half an hour later, Pamela felt much better. Jumping off the bed, she went into the bathroom to take a nice long bath. As she soaked in the tub filled with her favorite Rituals Organic Mandarin bath oil, she hummed Bob Marley's song, "No Woman, No Cry."

CHAPTER

30

A S THE DAYS TURNED INTO weeks and eventually months, Inga was about to give up hope of ever getting a reply from her parents. Then one night while she was in bed, checking her email, she saw a message from her mother in her inbox. Eagerly, she opened it. The message was simply the acronym: fyi... and an attached document. After downloading the file, Inga died a thousand deaths. Was this some cruel hoax by a hacker? This could not really be a message from her mother. Inga stared at the screen until her brain finally processed the information which claimed:

Lucas Erik Bengtsson, 60, beloved husband, brother and
friend, hastily left earthly life on October 21, 2011.
He's survived by his wife of 40 years
Hilda, and sister, Agnes Moller.
A private cremation service was held on
November 03, 2011 for family members.

Inga started having difficulty breathing and soon afterwards, began to shake. When she started feeling sharp pains in her chest, she screamed Khalid's name.

Inga didn't recall going to the ER of the hospital, or the physician attending to her for that matter. The only thing that she remembered was opening her eyes in a small, stark, hospital room when a petite Filipina nurse came to take her vital signs. Inga was relieved to see

Mother Abeer sitting on the lone reclining chair in the room. Since Inga was still in shock, the decision was made that she should be kept overnight at the hospital. The next morning, the physician, accompanied by another Filipina nurse, checked on her. Satisfied that she was in stable condition, he discharged her from the hospital.

As soon as Khalid picked Inga up from the hospital, she requested that he take her straight home. She needed to get to the bottom of that disturbing email. Upon arriving home, she immediately dialed her parents' telephone number. When her Aunt Agnes' voice came on the other end of the telephone line, Inga was certain that the shocking message was true. "Hello, hello???" said her aunt. Inga wanted to reply, but no matter how hard she tried, the words remained stuck in her throat. After the fifth, "He - Looo???" Inga's aunt hung up the phone. As Inga sat in a stupor, holding the telephone receiver to her ear, she couldn't help but wonder: Was she responsible for her father's demise?

Inga desperately wanted to fly home to Stockholm to see her mother. She wanted to hug and comfort her as they mourned together their common loss. She wanted her mother to know how very sorry she was for all the pain that she had caused them and ask for her forgiveness. Additionally, Inga wanted to reassure her mother that despite her new lifestyle, and the continents that physically separated them, she was still and would always be, her daughter. But somehow, Inga didn't think that her mother would welcome her with open arms. Her exclusion from the obituary, led her to believe that she had been disowned. *Perhaps, during the shock and confusion of my father's passing, my name had been accidentally omitted from his obituary,* Inga told herself. *Perhaps, for this same reason, I am only just being notified about his death, two months after his actual passing. And in such an impersonal way,* she rationalized.

However, being a logical thinker, Inga's left brain refused to let her off the hook with these feeble excuses. "Inga," it said, "get real!" And while she resented her mind's intrusion on the comfortable story that she was telling herself, in her heart of hearts, she knew that her left brain was right. So, reluctantly she confronted her accomplice Denial and gave herself a much-needed reality check: She was no longer her father's daughter. She was no longer her mother's child. She was now persona non-grata, the black sheep of the family.

As this truth sank in, and Inga owned it, a flood of conflicting emotions and thought-provoking questions assailed her very core. The most troubling being: If she had not fallen in love with Khalid, would her father still be alive? If she had broken the news of her engagement in a different way, would her father still be among the living? In her dark period of loss, Inga fell prey to all the Could haves, Should haves, and Would haves. On the brink of despair, she suddenly remembered the Buddhist meditation poem on fear that she had been introduced to while in Nepal. The poem encouraged one to "Sit" with his/her emotions in times of distress. And so, Inga gave herself permission to feel the whole spectrum of emotions bubbling up inside of her. Alternately, she sat with guilt...remorse... anger...anguish...fear and sadness. She sat with some of them more than once. At first reluctantly, but as she gradually connected with her inner self, acknowledged, and validated her feelings, Inga began to feel relief. Compassion and forgiveness were necessary for healing to occur. So, she worked on forgiving herself for all the things that she did or didn't say, or do to her dad, by writing him a letter. This act of writing to her father made her feel better and more connected to him.

Although she had started the healing process, at times, Inga felt bitter about her situation. By nature, she was a positive person; therefore, she planned to continue working on ridding herself of the bitterness in her soul. She understood that acidity corroded the vessel; and that negative energy did not serve her higher good. So, she hoped with time, this feeling of bitterness would pass. A playwright, whose name Inga had long forgotten, once wisely said, "In the end, all we can hope to end up with are the right regrets." This was Inga's fervent prayer for both her sake and her mother's too.

CHAPTER
31

AUREN'S ANNOUNCEMENT THAT SHE WAS dating Fred took Monica by surprise. It wasn't too long ago that Lauren had been eyeing another male colleague. But, as the saying goes, "If you can't be with the one you love, love the one you're with." Anyhow, Fred was a decent guy and he treated Lauren like a queen. So, Monica was happy for her friend. Naturally, since Lauren was now in a romantic relationship, she and Monica got together less frequently.

"Lady Lauren, long time no see," Monica quipped as Lauren entered her apartment after work one evening. Lauren flashed Monica her usual warm smile and plopped herself down on a chair in the living room. As was their routine, the friends spent half an hour venting about life in the Kingdom, their students' malicious evaluations of them, their students' lack of motivation, the nepotism, backstabbing and cliques pervasive on staff, then laughed at the absurdity of it all. "Daahling," Monica said in her best Southern drawl, "we really must write a book about this place someday – Unbelievable!" Lauren howled with laughter and shook her head. After their laughter subsided, Monica said, "I've been meaning to ask you, how's your buddy at the uni in Jeddah doing?"

"You mean Ralph? Honestly, I'm very concerned about him."

"Does he still cry himself to sleep each night?"

"Yep, he sure does. He is definitely depressed."

"I hope you don't mind me saying this Lauren, but if he's living in the most liberal city in the Kingdom, earning $60,000 USD

annually and crying himself to sleep each night, he really needs to move on. No job is worth so much unhappiness."

"Honey, I totally agree with you. I have suggested the very same thing to him on several occasions. This is his third year at the uni. He totally hates his job, but doesn't want to leave because the money is so good."

"Well, my friend, let's hope that he doesn't end up like that poor teacher in Riyadh who hung himself."

"Oh God no, don't say that, it would break my heart if Ralph was to commit suicide."

After chewing the fat several minutes more, Lauren rose from her seat. "Let me go now, I want to finish prepping for tomorrow's classes before Fred comes over." She slid her feet into her Birkenstock sandals. Then Monica accompanied Lauren to her front door. Lauren placed her right hand on the door knob then paused. The look on her face told Monica that her friend was trying to decide if she should say something or not. "Out with it," Monica coaxed. The pals exchanged a smile. Lauren became serious. She studied Monica's face for another minute before whispering, "Something big is going to go down tomorrow at work. Ciao!"

Later that night, Monica had a hard time falling asleep. She tossed and turned, and tried to guess what the "something" was that Lauren alluded to earlier. After what seemed like an eternity, her alarm clock finally went off. She jumped out of bed – eager to get the day started.

At lunchtime, one of the admins stopped by Lauren and Monica's office. She informed them that there would be a staff meeting later that day at the men's campus, immediately after their last class.

For the remainder of the workday, Monica's thoughts were preoccupied with the nature of this sudden meeting. She had a hard time concentrating on her lesson. Her students were also restless, so after they completed the exercises on the page, she decided to show them a Disney movie classic. Monica was relieved when the bell rang, signaling the end of class. "Banat!" she said, "for homework, please write a paragraph summarizing the movie." Some of Monica's students acknowledged her request with a nod of their heads; however, many of them merely grabbed their abayas and dashed out the door.

At the men's college, Monica spied Lauren and Fred sitting together in the auditorium where the staff meeting was going to be held. There was an empty seat nearby, so she took it. Their three coordinators: Lorie, Carly, and Mona, were standing on the platform with Edgar. From their facial expressions, it was obvious to all that this meeting intimately concerned them. Lorie had a look of stupor on her face, while a silly grin played across Carly's. Mona looked like she was about to burst into tears. Edgar cleared his throat; as if on cue, the room fell silent. "We have a lot of talent on staff," he stated. "I think that it's a good idea to give others the chance to develop their skills. So, effective today, I'm appointing three new colleagues in the role of coordinators at the female college." Monica casually glanced at Lauren. Their eyes locked, and Lauren smirked. Edgar continued, "Let's give a round of applause to the outgoing coordinators and a warm welcome to their replacements." The staff members all clapped mechanically, then filed out of the hall.

As was the norm in Saudi Arabia, the men got on one bus and the women boarded the other bus. The ride back to the compound was unusually quiet. There was none of the usual dialog or banter. The ex-coordinators all sat sullenly together in the rear of the bus, while their successors sat uncomfortably in the front.

When Monica alighted from the bus, she silently followed Lauren back to her flat. As soon as Lauren closed the door behind them, Monica asked, "What's really going on?" Lauren went through the usual motions of brewing tea. Monica kicked off her shoes and sat on the well-worn sofa with one leg tucked under her, while the other dangled over the edge of the sofa. After a while, the tea kettle stopped whistling. Lauren carefully poured the hot water over the Lipton green tea bags in the dainty tea cups which were a gift from Fred. She gently slid one of the tea cups and saucers over to Monica and sat down on the chair facing her friend. Exhaling slowly, Lauren stirred her tea with a spoon and took a sip. She frowned and got up for another packet of Sweet 'N Low. After adding the sweetener to her tea, she stirred it again. The suspense was killing Monica. "Well?" she impatiently prodded her pal. Lauren's green eyes twinkled mischievously, and she smiled smugly. Carefully, she raised her tea cup to her lips, and took another sip. She swallowed, then returned the cup to its saucer.

Rising from her seat, she walked over to her window and closed the window blinds. "This is very serious," Monica remarked. Lauren returned to her perch, sighed heavily and shook her head. Lowering her voice, she revealed, "Well, many teachers on Lorie's team were unhappy with her because she does a lot of micromanaging...Carly was overheard - through the classroom walls by some of our peers on several occasions - giving her students extra time on their exams, AND, also giving them the answers to some questions...Mona was busted for having illicit sex with Lover-boy. I mean she was literally caught in mid-stroke with Lover-boy. Her husband's back in Canada on emergency leave visiting his gravely ill father." With each of Lauren's revelations, Monica's eyes got bigger and bigger.

"Whaat! I thought that Lover-boy was romantically involved with Doreen," Monica uttered softly.

"That's right," Lauren replied. "I feel so sorry for Doreen, she's such a sweetie-pie."

"Did Lover-boy also get a penalty?"

Lauren picked up her cup and took another sip of tea before she answered, "Kinda, sorta. He won't be able to renew his contract."

Shaking her head, Monica helped herself to two oatmeal raisin cookies on Lauren's kitchen counter. "What's the matter with these people? Did they come to Saudi Arabia this stupid, or is Saudi

Arabia to blame for their stupidity?" she asked rhetorically. "This makes no sense."

Lauren roared with laughter. "Yeah, these people are something else," she replied after she had caught her breath.

A few minutes later, Monica looked at her watch and rose reluctantly. She grabbed another cookie then picked up her belongings. On her way out the door, she mumbled, "Seriously Lauren, we really need to write a book about this place."

CHAPTER

32

YASMIN ROSE SLOWLY FROM HER chair and walked into her bedroom. Moving over to the full-length beveled mirror on the door of her wardrobe, she inspected her face carefully. It was still striking, but the dark circles under her eyes, despite getting six hours of sleep nightly, made her look older than her twenty-eight years. Next, Yasmin studied her body. Her arms could do with a bit of toning, ditto her thighs. Yep, it was definitely time for her to improve her diet and exercise routine. Sighing loudly, she changed into her modest workout gear. After wrapping her scarf around her head, she stretched and went for a walk.

As Yasmin finished the last lap of her walk, she spied Lydia leaving the small convenience store on the compound. Lydia was carrying several empty boxes. Yasmin quickened her steps and overtook her pal. "It looks like you're getting ready to do some packing," she said to her.

"That's right," Lydia replied with her usual cool self. "It's time to go. Home sweet home, here I come!"

Although Lydia still wore her poker face, Yasmin was positive that Lydia was devastated by the incident at the college two days ago. On Monday, at break time, Lydia had accidentally left her handbag in the classroom. When she returned after the break, she was greeted with the message "Fu*k you, Lydia!" scrawled on the whiteboard. To add insult to injury, 50 riyals had been stolen from her purse. Although she had reported the incident to the dean, no action had been taken.

"I don't blame you," Yasmin said softly, "but why don't you just hang in there? The trimester is almost over, and we'll get that sweet bonus as a reward for all our troubles."

"Money isn't everything," Lydia replied sharply. "There's no way after what happened to me that I'm going to continue working in this place! I deserve better."

"Do you suspect that one of your students did it?"

"Of course," Lydia snapped. "A colleague isn't going to risk her job for the equivalent of $13 USD."

"Good point that would indeed be daft. Do you need a hand with packing?"

Lydia graced Yasmin with her rare smile and replied, "Thanks, but I have everything under control."

But of course, you do, why am I not surprised? Yasmin thought to herself. "When's your flight?"

"Soon," Lydia replied tersely.

Yasmin had a sneaking suspicion that her mate planned to do a runner. "Well, it was nice knowing you," she said to her in parting. "If I don't see you again, take care."

Although Yasmin never got to know Lydia as well as she wanted to, she was indeed going to miss her. In a strange way, just from lounging together by the swimming pool, Yasmin had felt connected to her.

CHAPTER

33

O F COURSE, BEING AN ONLY child, I knew quite well
the importance of keeping the family line going. Having
said that, I must confess that I never felt a biological need to have
children. Don't get me wrong, I adore little people and think they
are cute. However, as you already know, prior to falling in love with
Khalid, I was very career-oriented. My plan was to quickly move up
the corporate ladder at an acclaimed international accounting firm.
Then later, when I had acquired sufficient work experience and saved
enough money, open my own company. As such, I never really gave
motherhood and parenting much thought. Frankly speaking, the
idea of having to actively parent for at least eighteen years of my life
just seemed like a job for which I wasn't really cut out for or qualified
to do. Despite being in my late twenties, I was still a big kid at heart
and not particularly keen on undertaking the huge responsibility of
providing for the emotional, physical, and financial needs of infants.
Heck, I find it challenging enough attending to my own needs. The
thought of being deprived of countless hours of beauty sleep, having
to change diapers, contending with noise and restrictions on my
mobility and lifestyle because of motherhood, simply did not appeal
to me. I know that this might sound selfish to some of you, and I
can understand your point of view. However, this is honestly how I
felt prior to becoming a mother.

Despite the souring of my relationship with my parents, I must
give them credit for never having pressured me to get married and
procreate. Whether they secretly desired to become grandparents

someday or not, they never once hinted this to me. Instead, they always encouraged me to live my life to the fullest and on my own terms. This way, they said, I would avoid having regrets, both of a personal and a professional nature, when I had come to the end of my journey.

Now, I have several friends from college who are happily juggling marriage life, parenting, and careers. And I tip my hat to them. On the other hand, I'm acquainted with many couples who rushed into having kids because they figured it was the right thing for them to do, or felt pressured to start a family because of other people's expectations of them, and ended up feeling burdened by their children. *Thanks, but no thanks – I'll pass*, was my sentiment on the matter for quite a long time.

Even though my marriage took me by surprise and I am for the most part, contentedly married, I still didn't really give motherhood much thought. Of course, I knew that the day would come when Khalid and his relatives would have expectations of us fulfilling the obligation of providing an heir. However, since Khalid and I were newly-wed, and just getting the opportunity to really know each other, conversations about planned parenting hadn't even occurred. So, when the obstetrician informed me a few months into my marriage that I was pregnant, I felt ambivalent about motherhood.

In contrast, Khalid was ecstatic when he learned that he was going to be a father and immediately relayed the news to his parents. You can well imagine that I was a nervous wreck! My days and nights were spent worrying about my soon to be new role as mommy. The realization that I would be bringing into this world not one, but TWO children at the same time, was very scary to me. Oh, how I wished that my mother and I were on speaking terms and I could have confided in her my angst over my situation. I would have loved to be able to have mother-daughter talks with her about her own pregnancy, for her to tell me exactly what I could expect during mine, give me tips about proper nutrition, exercise, stretch marks, morning sickness, and labor pains. Most of all, I wanted her reassurance that everything was going to be alright.

I would have given anything to have my mother back in my life. For her to accept me, my husband, our kids, and in-laws as her family. For her to relish her new role as grand-ma. It would have been lovely to have her rejoice with us and take part in the baby-welcoming ceremony. Also, it would have been wonderful for her to come and stay with me during this trying period in my life. I think that we would have had fun decorating the nursery together and shopping for baby clothes at Mumzworld. More importantly, it would have been a great opportunity for us to rekindle our relationship; and, for my mom to get to know Khalid, Mother Abeer, and Dr. Mahmood personally. We could then put our differences aside and work together to raise the next generation in a loving and nurturing environment. But of course, these wishes of mine were purely wishful thinking on my part.

Since my mother had washed her hands of me, and clearly wanted nothing to do with Khalid and his family, I could not bring myself to notify her that she was going to become a grand-mother. Considering the sad and precarious state of our relationship, I thought it best to keep her in the dark about my pregnancy. Heaven forbid, this condition be the cause of her demise. Right or wrong, I still felt somewhat responsible for my father's untimely death. Suffice to say, I relied heavily on Mother Abeer for guidance and support during my pregnancy and after my children's birth. Likewise, following the delivery of my beautiful sons, she has continued to be an integral part of their lives. So, despite our differences, for these reasons, I am eternally indebted to her.

When the midwife placed my sons in my arms for the first time, all doubts and fears that I had harbored about motherhood instantaneously evaporated. As I marveled at their innocence and cuddled them, I made a pledge that I would be the very best role model they could ever have, and I would love them unconditionally.

Keeping with cultural tradition, Khalid had the honor of choosing our children's names since they are males. He decided to name our first-born Mahmood, after his father. Our second son, he named Muhammad, in honor of the prophet (PBUH). It so happened that Mahmood inherited my thick, curly blonde hair, while Muhammad has my dad's square jaw.

I'm relieved that Mother Abeer and Dr. Mahmood dote on Mahmood and Muhammad. They seem to relish the times that they spend with their grand kids and vice versa. Weekend trips to the park, the oral telling of Nawadir, and painting sessions, are a few of the bonding activities that my sons delight in doing with their grandparents. Sometimes, I can't help but wonder how I'll respond to them when they get older and start asking questions about my side of the family tree and heritage. When I would get all worked up in trying to come up with solutions to this potential problem, Khalid with his usual rational and sensible self, reassured me that, "We'll figure out how to cross that river when we get to it."

I'm making the most of my new role as mom. And am doing my best as nurturer and educator. As much as possible, I try to shield Mahmood and Muhammad from the unpleasantness of life. So, I'm currently homeschooling them. Mother Abeer said that when they get older, they must continue their education in London. We all know how swiftly the years fly! Before I know it, my boys will be out on their own, trying to make their way in the world. I try hard not to worry about how kind or cruel the world will be to them due to their dual ethnic heritage, nationality, and religion. Time will tell. It's easier said than done, but I'm trying my best to live only in the present and enjoy, as much as possible, these precious moments with my boys.

CHAPTER

34

MONICA WAS SO GLAD THAT she had accepted Yasmin's dinner invitation. Yasmin had turned out to be a really fun person to hang out with. It was nice for Monica to have somebody to socialize with off the compound. She hated living in a fishbowl, where her colleagues' faces were the first and the last things that she saw each time she left her apartment. Working and living so closely with them made it hard to keep the professional and personal separate. She suspected that was the reason why there were so many incidences of improprieties occurring on the compound. Some of her colleagues just did not understand boundaries.

There's a saying, "birds of a feather will flock together," and this was indeed the case for Monica and her peers. Once people settled into cliques, they established their turf. So, the "wild ones" hung out around the swimming pool. The shisha smokers congregated on their ring leader's stoop, and the vegans/yoga enthusiasts socialized on their guru's balcony. They had all fallen into the comfortable daily routine of hanging out with the same people, in the same spot, after work. This was not Monica's style. Therefore, she preferred to keep her own counsel. Aside from Lauren, she seldom socialized with her other co-workers. Apart from the job and the air that they breathed, Monica and her colleagues had nothing else in common. Quite frankly, with all the nonsense that had been going on, she thought that keeping to herself was the best policy. She had witnessed too many of her peers being thrown under the bus by their so-called buddies. When the weather was pleasant, Monica liked to sit on her little balcony and observe the scene. She found it interesting to watch the dynamics between her peers. Some of the bonds seemed a bit odd to her; and she wondered, would these people have associated with each other if they were in their homelands?

Monica and Yasmin clicked instantly because they shared several interests: spirituality, reading self-development books, and eating spicy food. So, Monica found it refreshing to be able to connect with somebody on these topics instead of the usual work-related ones. When Monica closed shop, she liked to leave the business of work behind. She didn't want to be on the compound continuously engaged in mindless talk about work. As soon as she had finished prepping for the next day's lessons, she switched off work mode. Yasmin felt the same way about her work environment, so she and Monica got on splendidly. Of course, they were not above swapping tales about their workday. Like Monica, Yasmin worked with a mixed-bag of colleagues; therefore, there was always some juicy gossip to share.

As a rule, Monica didn't like to travel with companions because it complicated matters. Somebody was usually running late, or wanting to change plans mid-trip; that was why she preferred to travel solo. However, since she and Yasmin had so much in common, Monica made an exception to her rule for their upcoming mid-term break. She and Yasmin had a five-day break at the beginning of January and were going to Bahrain. They booked rooms at the Nomads' Nest and planned to share the taxi ride to Manama. Since things were quite hectic at their respective institutions, the women wouldn't see each other prior to their school break. So, both were highly looking forward to their reunion and unwinding in beautiful Bahrain.

Seriously now, how can anyone __not__ love Bahrain? Monica wondered as the customs officer stamped her passport at the border. *It is such a vibrant little country!* With world-class dining, shopping, and entertainment galore, it was a typical western expat's idea of paradise. Too bad the cost of living was so high and salaries much lower than in Saudi Arabia. If it weren't for these factors, Monica would actively seek employment in Manama.

While Bahrain is hands down the most liberal and tolerant Arab state in the Gulf region, it had two contradictions that baffled Monica. The first one personally affected her because she is a movie buff. The second, which was prostitution, affected her only indirectly. In the past, whenever Monica came to Bahrain for a weekend getaway, she would automatically go to the cinema and spend half of her Friday watching the latest Western or Bollywood action movies. Now, she didn't bother going to the cinema anymore because all the romantic scenes had been edited out of the films. This struck Monica as rather hypocritical when she thought about Bahrain's embarrassing reputation of being an oasis of debauchery, and the Middle East's top destination for sex tourism. Try as she might, she couldn't wrap her head around the fact that prostitution, although illegal in Bahrain, is tolerated and highly visible; while love scenes on the silver screen are censored.

The Thursday afternoon that Monica and Yasmin departed Al-Khobar for Bahrain, traffic was horrendous. Vehicles were bumper-to-bumper on the causeway as both Saudi men and expats alike made the jaunt across the border to freedom. Yasmin was exhausted. It had been a rough week for her. So, she decided to take a nap, since it was at least another hour's drive to their lodging. In the interim, Monica entertained herself by engaging in some people-watching. She noticed that once motorists crossed over to Bahrain, the somber atmosphere changed. Car stereos became audible and female passengers took off their veils and abayas. Monica was amused when a burgundy colored Maserati sports car overtook her vehicle. The young Saudi behind the wheel, bobbed his head from side to side, as a rapper's husky voice blared out from the car's window, "Yeah, we've come to party!" As they rounded another bend, she saw several vehicles pulled over to the side of the road. The occupants, all Saudi motorists, had shed their thobes. Monica smirked. "*Hmph! Phony fuckers,*" she muttered, sotto voce. There was no doubt in her mind that it was bacchanal time for those men. They had come to carouse and have a good time with the women in the flesh trade. She was willing to bet her paycheck that they wouldn't see the interior of any mosque during their stay in Bahrain.

While Monica had not conducted any scientific research on her hypothesis, from her observations, the Saudi men in general, preferred to play with the fairer ladies-of-the-night, so the Russian courtesans did very well. Expat men, on the other hand, tended to gravitate towards the Filipina and Chinese prostitutes. Her mind flashed on her ex-colleague Paul, who was recently terminated from the university. According to the word on the compound, Paul had been experiencing flu-like illness - chills followed by a fever - for a month. So, he eventually went to the hospital for a check-up. He was devastated when medical tests revealed that he was HIV positive. As Paul had not traveled back to Wisconsin since his arrival in Saudi Arabia, and he frequently traveled to Manama on weekends, tongues wagged that he had contracted that dreadful disease in Bahrain. Monica wondered how he planned to break the news to his poor wife that he was fired and HIV positive. These reflections led her to ponder the rate of HIV and AIDS in Saudi Arabia. She would love to know the statistics for Saudi males who patronize prostitutes; but had a feeling that such research findings would never be publicized.

Two hours later, the taxi finally arrived at the Nomads' Nest. Just as the taxi pulled up in front of the hotel, Monica woke Yasmin up. "Honey, we're home," she said to her and grinned. The Nomads' Nest was Monica's favorite retreat from the lunacy and oppressiveness of Saudi Arabia. It was a boutique hotel located by the corniche. It had outstanding amenities and services for clients interested in health and wellness. One such service that Monica liked was their evening turndown service; it included little Patchi chocolate treats being left on the NN monogrammed white pillowcases on her bed. She felt like royalty. Whenever Monica stayed at the Nomad's Nest, without fail, she always treated herself to one or two sessions of aromatherapy massage and foot reflexology. She also enjoyed relaxing in the sauna and jacuzzi.

The proprietor was a middle-aged Briton, who had formerly been an expat in Saudi Arabia. According to the hotel's receptionist, who Monica had a good rapport with, back in the day, the hotelier, like current expats in Saudi Arabia, would come to Bahrain for some rest and relaxation. On one such trip, he met his future wife, a local named Basma. He needed directions to the Al Fateh Grand Mosque and one thing led to another. Now, here they were, a decade later, the proud owners of this fabulous Zen-like property.

The reception team greeted Monica and Yasmin with a customary smile and complimentary glass of fresh watermelon juice. After receiving their room keys, they made plans to meet for brunch the following morning at eleven and called it a day.

Monica smiled as she opened the door to her suite. A large, black lacquered console table stood near the door. On it sat a solitary, medium-sized, cylindrical shaped white vase. In the vase were a bunch of Cherry Blossom fragrance sticks that emitted a divine scent. She inhaled deeply, allowing the aroma to soothe her. She walked unhurriedly into the bedroom. In the middle of the room, a magnificent wooden partition screen of carved encircled diamonds stood sentinel behind the bed. Across from the foot of the bed was a bamboo chest of drawers. Monica ambled over to it and unpacked her travel bag. After a quick shower, she sank under the crisp bed sheets and fell into Morpheus' warm embrace.

One of the things that Monica loved about Bahrain was the freedom expats enjoyed dressing as they pleased. Admittedly, some female expats took this liberty too far; their attire left nothing to the imagination. Nonetheless, Monica found it liberating not to have to put on the abaya in Bahrain if she wasn't in the mood to wear it. It was a wonderful feeling for her to see her arms and legs again in public. So, for her brunch date with Yasmin, she wore her tangerine colored, sleeveless, knee-length dress with platform shoes. *"If the*

Mutawah could only see me now," Monica murmured to herself as she assessed her appearance in the full-length mirror in the hallway. Quite pleased with her reflection, she blew it a kiss. After locking the door to her room, she went to wait for Yasmin in the hotel's restaurant.

While waiting for Yasmin to arrive, Monica decided to read the hotel's complimentary international newspaper. Idly, she flipped through the paper to the section filled with news reports about Saudi Arabia. *Former Hindu inmate sentenced to a seven-year jail sentence, 2,100 lashes and 30,000 riyals fine, pardoned after converting to Islam. Thousands of Filipino expats employed at a Saudi construction company, without wages for six months, beg the Philippine embassy to intervene. Gay Saudi prince who beat and strangled his Sudanese manservant to death will be extradited to Saudi Arabia to finish his life sentence.* Against Monica's better judgement, she scanned the CCTV images captured of the prince in the hotel's lift, striking his defenseless servant. She began to see red as she read the article detailing the prince's sexual abuse of his servant over the years and the pampered treatment he received while in a British prison. Ironically, in his homeland, the prince would not stand trial for murder, but for the unacceptable act of homosexuality. The prince, no doubt, due to his social status, would escape the usual fate of a homosexual which is a public execution (by beheading) at Deera Square in Riyadh. *Ahh, the privilege of Wasta*, Monica sighed ruefully as she folded the newspaper and took a sip of water.

For obvious reasons, most Saudi expats referred to Deera Square as "Chop, Chop Square." It had been the site of many executions of both expats and locals alike for crimes that the international community found controversial: adultery, armed robbery, drug use and trafficking, murder, rape, and renouncing Islam. Previously, these executions were held on Friday after noon prayers. Now, they occurred at nine o'clock in the morning, on any given day of the week.

Monica blocked the newspaper's troubling reports from her mind when she heard Yasmin's voice. "Good morning, Monica! Sorry to keep you waiting."

"No worries, girlfriend. Actually, you're right on time. How did you sleep last night?"

"Alright, but the guests' baby in the room next to mine cried constantly throughout the night. So, I ended up having to sleep with my earplugs."

"Oh no, what a bummer, fingers crossed you'll sleep better tonight."

"Thanks, luv… Shall we have a look at the food items on the buffet table?"

There was an exotic array of halal Asian and Mediterranean-inspired dishes, Western grilled meats, an eye-popping selection of seafood, a smorgasbord of soups, salads, bread/rolls, cheese, and a tempting selection of traditional Middle Eastern pastries spread across five long tables on one side of the dining room. After piling their plates with morsels from each platter and bowl, the pals returned to their table. While eating, they had a good time swapping stories about all the mindboggling and ridiculous things that had been going on at their respective workplaces. "So, at Christmas time, which you already know us Muslims don't celebrate," said Yasmin warming up to her tale, "Our thoughtful boss gifted each staff member, including us Muslims, with a rum cake." Monica's jaw dropped in disbelief. "A rum cake. You must be joking! How did she manage to smuggle them into the country? Only in Saudi Arabia," she laughed long and heartily; then wiped the tears from her eyes caused from laughing too hard.

On their second trip to the buffet table, the line was considerably longer. While they waited in the queue, they heard a male voice behind them order the waitstaff to bring more mimosa cocktails to the drink station. The voice, Monica knew that nasal-sounding voice. She thought hard as to where she had heard it before. At the same time, Yasmin's stomach lurched. She had also recognized that voice. Could it be? No, it couldn't. He wouldn't make such a request. Or, would he?

Monica, unable to place the speaker, casually, turned around to see who had spoken. "Well, Abdul, fancy running into you here!" she exclaimed. Abdul, who had his right arm draped protectively over a pretty Filipina's shoulder, clearly wasn't thrilled to see her.

Yasmin felt an increasing tightness in her chest and her breath became ragged. Slowly, she turned around. She gasped when she saw her older, married cousin and his unsavory playmate. Abdul's eyes bulged when he recognized his cousin. He immediately detached himself from his paramour. Yasmin ignored her cousin's partner and addressed him in Urdu. "Salaam, Chacha-zaad Bhai. How's your health? How's your father? How are your sons?" Composing himself, Abdul managed a weak smile and replied, "Salaam, cousin Yasmin. My family and I are fine, thank you for asking. How is your father? How are your brothers?" The mounting tension between the cousins was discomfiting. So, Monica hurriedly selected some desserts from the buffet and returned to her table. Yasmin managed a faint smile, and replied, "Take care, cousin Abdul. I'll be sure to tell my father that I saw you."

Without waiting for Abdul to reply, she walked purposefully back to her table empty-handed. "Oh Yasmin, I'm <u>so</u> sorry about this. Do you want to talk?" Monica asked. Yasmin's face was hard, and her gaze was fixed straight ahead. She shook her head and sat stonily at the table. After a while, she spoke, "May I ask how you know Abdul?"

"He's my colleague and we live on the same compound," Monica replied.

Yasmin was tempted to ask Monica about her cousin's behavior, but resisted the urge. She didn't really want to discuss such delicate matters with her buddy. After Monica finished eating, Yasmin told her that she had decided to return to Al Khobar the next day. While Monica was disappointed, she understood Yasmin's decision. She admired her ability to remain so calm and collected under

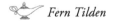

the circumstances. She knew that if she were in Yasmin's shoes, she would not have handled the situation so graciously. Lightly squeezing Yasmin's hand, Monica said, "I understand my friend. Know that I'm here for you."

As penance for overeating, Monica decided to stretch her legs around the corniche. The weather was balmy, further adding to the enjoyment of her walk. As she strolled back towards the Nomads' Nest, she reflected on the earlier drama at the restaurant. *Who'd of thunk it, Mr. Casanova has a woman in Bahrain and was busted by his own cousin. Talk about being fucked up!* At the compound, Abdul always presented himself as an upright, pious Muslim, happily married with two kids back in Scotland. Monica would never have suspected him of indulging in alcohol and infidelity. While the matter was quite serious, the situation struck her as rather droll and she burst out laughing; not giving a damn if fellow passersby thought she was crazy.

CHAPTER

35

ALTHOUGH IT'S COMMON KNOWLEDGE THAT some Pakistani men will have extramarital affairs, it still broke Yasmin's heart to know that her own cousin, Abdul, would be guilty of this offense. *How long had he been cheating on cousin Taiba?* she wondered. While she didn't condone Abdul's behavior, she was grateful that he at least had enough respect for his wife to mess around on another continent.

It certainly could be a whole lot worse. There was a lovely neighbor who Yasmin grew up calling auntie, who is married to a womanizer. She doesn't know how auntie does it, but she gracefully suffers the indignities of her husband's infidelity daily. Auntie knew about the other woman for years, but looked the other way because her spouse continued to take care of his financial obligations to both her and their children. However, when he married his foreign mistress and brought her to live with them, auntie could no longer deny the reality of his indiscretions. And so, she became the laughing stock of their community. Talk about the ultimate slap in the face! Regardless, auntie continues to attend to all her wifely duties just as she did at the start of their union.

The institution of marriage is one that Yasmin takes very seriously. Daily, she prays to Allah that when she gets married, her husband will honor her and their union. And if he doesn't, Yasmin hopes that she will have auntie's strength and grace to remain committed to him and forgive him. One of the tenets of the Islamic tradition is the importance of forgiveness. If one desires to

be forgiven for his transgressions, he must learn to forgive others. Especially, if one seeks forgiveness from God, he should learn to forgive others for their offenses. Since Yasmin strives to be a better Muslim, she is trying to find it in her heart to pardon Abdul for his transgressions. So, next salat, she will make dua for him.

CHAPTER

36

JUST FOR OLD TIMES' SAKE, Pamela donned her abaya and took one final stroll around her neighborhood. She smiled as she saw the luxury cars on King Abdullaziz Highway motor by. When she and Glenn had first arrived in the Kingdom, they had enjoyed playing a little game of seeing who could spot the most Ferraris, Lamborghinis, Jaguars, and Porsches on their nightly strolls. Gradually, the novelty wore off, since seeing these cars became commonplace.

She sat on one of the lovely stone benches lining the highway and watched the vehicles whiz by. Two middle-aged men clad in t-shirts and sweatpants, jogged past her. Pamela wondered about their domestic life. It was a more pleasant diversion to think about their affairs instead of her own sad circumstances. As the sun began to set, Pamela detected a drop in the temperature. Reluctantly, she stood up, and walked back towards Salam camp. While waiting to cross the street, she spied a sleek, cream colored car gliding towards her. She grinned as she spotted the unmistakable Phantom on the hood. *Sweet!* She wished that Glenn was here to share the moment with her. *"Oh well, I suppose he'll have other opportunities to see a Rolls Royce for himself,"* she said aloud.

Back in her villa, Pamela sat down at Glenn's elegant ebony desk which they had shipped from Tanzania. She smiled at their wedding photo tastefully displayed in a Waterford Crystal frame on top of the desk. She couldn't help but think how nice it would have been to have kids inherit these beautiful treasures. Gently, she picked up the frame and brought it close to her face. She studied her younger self; her photo registered her elation and optimism for her and Glenn's bright future together. Next, she looked at Glenn's image. His eyes and broad smile also reflected his joy and anticipation of the journey they were about to embark on.

They had met at a McGill Exchange Student Association welcome party event during FROSH/Orientation week. Pamela had been sitting quietly at one of the plastic tables in the rear of the room when Glenn had approached and asked permission to join her. His deep voice and adorable puppy eyes had captivated her. His strong Caribbean accent charmed her, and she would eventually grow to hang on his every word. He was the perfect gentleman and had bought her a couple of drinks throughout the night. When the DJ played the reggae song, "Here Comes the Hot Stepper," and Glenn asked Pamela to dance, she had felt a tingling sensation through their molecular connection. He blew her away with his smooth dance moves which she tried to match by swinging her arms and hips to the "ridim." When the song was over, he had shyly asked for her dorm room number. Feelings were mutual, so without hesitating, Pamela had given it to him.

Although she hadn't really thought much about getting her Mrs. along with her BEng degree, that night, Pamela had fantasized what it would be like to be called Mrs. Glenn Huxtable. "Mrs. Glenn Huxtable," she had liked the sound of it. Truth be told, she still liked being called Mrs. Glenn Huxtable. And, she was quite proud to be known as Glenn's wife. He was a remarkable man who had achieved a lot. Furthermore, he had introduced her to a beautiful and exciting world. Due to him, over the years, Pamela had met many interesting people and tried different activities which she wouldn't have had the courage to do on her own.

She remembered how wonderful and attentive he was to her when she was going through culture shock during the first three months of her arrival in the Kingdom. His patience with her during those bleak days when she was being very negative. He would always tell her that, "their gain would outweigh their pain," and, "they're going to pull through this together." Despite bringing work home from the office, Glenn always made time to eat dinner with her and strolled with her around their neighborhood each night. Also, he had gotten his office mates to encourage their wives to include Pamela in their circle, which greatly helped her adjust to this strange culture.

Fond memories of the time that they did the Tandem Bungee Jump together at Gravity Zone in Dubai crossed her mind. Pamela had been terrified, and balked when instructed to jump. Her legs had become rigid and immobilized. It took a lot of coaxing from Glenn and faith in him to get her to jump. At first, it all seemed surreal as they were free falling through the air. Time seemed to stand still as they hung upside down and looked at the Burj Khalifa in the backdrop. Pamela felt both a sense of peace and a rush of euphoria at that moment. All too soon, it was over.

Then, there was the first time that they went sand dune bashing in Abu Dhabi. Pamela almost threw up when their Toyota Land Cruiser bounced all over the striking golden dunes of the Arabian Desert. Gripping the roll bar above her head tightly as their 4X4 fishtailed, and bashed the huge, steep sand dunes, Pamela had screamed and cussed like a sailor. Her behavior had greatly amused Glenn. Once she began to relax and was confident that their vehicle wouldn't tip over, Pamela squealed with excitement.

Being a romantic, she found the natural beauty of the desert quite stunning. Bathed in the soft light of the setting sun, the landscape looked magnificent and provided them with many Nikon memories. Like their bungee jump, this adventure had given Pamela an adrenaline rush that she would never forget. It had also strengthened her bond with Glenn. There was no denying that he was her Rock of Gibraltar.

Very gingerly, Pamela returned the frame to its place at the upper right corner of the desk. *We've come a long way, baby*, she thought wistfully. Bending down, she pulled out a sheaf of personalized stationery from her carry-on bag. After fifteen minutes, she had

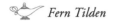 *Fern Tilden*

ordered her thoughts and was finally ready to write them down. Borrowing the Montblanc pen that she had given to Glenn for his last birthday, she scribbled:

> *Love of my Life,*
>
> *Thanks for such an incredible journey. It has been one helluva ride!*
>
> *If you change your mind about having kids, do let me know.*

Pamela pressed the paper to her lips and placed it on Glenn's pillow. She struggled to pull her wedding ring off her finger. Holding it between her fingers, she looked at it for a minute, then put it back on.

There was still one hour left before the taxi was scheduled to pick her up. Pamela pondered whether to telephone Angel to say goodbye. Logic won, and she resisted the temptation. Instead, she flipped through her photo albums, looking at all the beautiful memories that she and Glenn had created.

CHAPTER
37

YASMIN HUNG UP THE PHONE and slumped back in her chair with a loud sigh. For the past month, every time she had called home, she has had to endure her mother's nagging reminders that her sell-by date was fast approaching; and it was time for her to settle down and start a family before it was too late. "Beta, I just sent your photo to my friend Lubna in London," Yasmin's mother told her during their last conversation. "Her son is thirty-five years old and an engineer." As her mother's parting words sank in, Yasmin glanced at her body and cringed. It was time for her to get busy with an exercise routine.

She really couldn't complain; her parents had been very liberal and patient with her. They had allowed her to complete her higher education, live on campus during that period, and later, embark on a career, before pressuring her about marriage. Many of her peers weren't as fortunate. Even before they had earned their bachelor's degree, their mothers were on the prowl for suitors. Although Yasmin's parents weren't thrilled with her decision to work in Saudi Arabia, they had still given her their blessings. So, now that her contract was coming to an end, it was only reasonable that their expectations of her getting married be met. After all, her older sister Khirad, was already married and her younger sister, Alishbah, was engaged.

Where does the time go? Yasmin wondered aloud as she looked at her calendar. There were exactly sixty days remaining to the end of her contract. "*I need to get it together. Fast!*" she exclaimed.

Yasmin sighed heavily, and tilted her head back. Closing her eyes, she inhaled and exhaled deeply three times. Memories surrounding the unpleasantness of Khirad's first matchmaking experience surfaced. When their mother was shopping around for a suitable husband for her sister, their mother's first choice of a mate was a highly educated Pakistani-Briton from an affluent family. After exchanging photos with the eligible bachelor's mother, their mother was bluntly told that, "Khirad's too dark-skinned to be considered." *Who needs that humiliation?* Yasmin thought as she opened her eyes. It took her mother almost one year to arrange Khirad's union to Sadiq, but her good judgement and perseverance paid off. Sadiq and Khirad have been married almost seven years.

Next, Yasmin recalled Khirad's beautiful wedding reception at the spacious reception hall in their hometown. Khirad looked absolutely radiant in a crimson-color designer lengha choli. Her makeup and mehndi were professionally applied; and her classic jewelry, compliments of Sadiq. The food was exquisitely catered; all in all, the event was a lovely affair and no expense was spared. These memories led Yasmin to daydream about her own nuptials. She wouldn't want a function as elaborate as Khirad's; instead, she would prefer to have a small, intimate wedding with only close family members and friends. Keeping it simple would also leave more funds available for a down payment on a flat.

Yasmin was happy that Khirad and Sadiq seemed quite compatible with each other and they appeared to have a wonderful marriage. He was a good provider and very respectful of her sister. More importantly, though, they shared the same sense of humor and core values. Although Sadiq would not be considered handsome, he did have what was called a winning personality and was highly regarded in their community. Yasmin also admired the fact that her brother-in-law was supportive of Khirad's desire to work part-time. In general, Pakistani men are conservative and discouraged their wives from working outside the home. So, Yasmin hoped that her husband would be equally as flexible as Sadiq because she wanted to continue her career.

Although her personal experience with men was limited to brief, superficial exchanges, Yasmin had a pretty clear idea of what she deserved in a mate and wanted in her marriage. From observing her father's treatment of her mother, and likewise her brother-in-law's conduct towards her big sister, she knew that the most important qualities of a good husband were faithfulness to Allah, maturity, good character, and financial stability. Using their behavior as the criterion for evaluating her future groom, Yasmin desired a spouse who was open-minded, plus her intellectual, and social equal.

My mother has her work cut out for her, she murmured to herself. Studies indicated that most Pakistani-Briton men tended not to be as educated or financially secure as their female counterparts. Since their culture was a patriarchal one, those men felt threatened in their manhood and usually ended up marrying a woman who was inferior to them. So, with the encouragement of their families, they preferred to seek brides from the motherland.

Another reason why middle-class Pakistani-Briton women like Yasmin have difficulty finding eligible mates is because their male counterparts tend to marry outside of their culture and race. Since the Qur'an permits Muslim men to wed women of the Christian and Jewish faiths, this situation creates a lot of friction and resentment among the Muslim women because the men who are "a better catch," are the ones who tend to leave their community. Due to this shortage of ideal men, one of Yasmin's best friends, her name's Ikram and she's a dentist, last year, traveled to Glasgow to find a husband at a Muslim marriage event. Sad, but true! Yasmin hoped that she wouldn't have to do the same.

Right or wrong, she strongly believes that every successful Pakistani-Briton man has a moral obligation to marry within his race. While Yasmin doesn't have a problem with interracial unions per se, from her personal observations, these interracial, intercultural marriages become overly complicated and usually don't work out.

It was a fact that her fellow countrymen who married women from different cultures and religions had a lot more difficulties to contend with in their households. For instance, cultural acceptance by in-laws and religious misunderstandings were rife. As far as Yasmin was concerned, all this additional stress and problems just isn't worth it. Besides, if all the good Pakistani-Briton men take foreign wives, what will become of their rich heritage? How will future generations know about, and appreciate, their past?

CHAPTER

38

TODAY IS ONE OF THOSE days that Monica just feels like saying, "Fuck it!" Although she still had two months remaining to the end of her contract, she was already beginning to feel that it was time for her to move on. Everybody and everything was beginning to grate on her nerves. She was losing patience with the locals who innocently inquired if she was an "original" American. They were under the impression that all true Americans only came in one color - white. At the malls, the children's constant gawking was also beginning to get under her skin. She had to seriously fight the puerile temptation to stick her tongue out at them.

Furthermore, Monica has had enough of the unrelenting heat. Being drenched in sweat the minute she stepped outdoors was getting old. Worse, the heat was doing some serious damage to her hair and skin. Despite conditioning her hair regularly, it was always dry and the texture of straw. Ditto her skin, which prior to coming to the Kingdom had been normal. Since her arrival, her skin had become ashy. It was so dry, it made a mockery of her body lotion's "24-hour moisture" claim.

On the job, it was becoming increasingly difficult for her to be genuinely pleasant to some of her peers. She had never been good at being phony. Having intimate knowledge about her colleagues and their backstabbing ways, Monica had lost respect for many of them. Throughout the workday, she had to force herself to wear a smile on her face. In staff meetings when some of the BS artists were trying to make themselves look good, it took all of her willpower to remain silent and play along with them. The games were becoming more malicious as people strove to curry favor with the boss at the expense of their "friends" and she really wanted no part of that mess.

Monica never thought that the day would come when she would say the following, but she was finally beginning to feel that many of her peers, whose mantra was "do the bare minimum at work," have had the right attitude all along. This was a hard pill for her to swallow because she had never been that kind of a person. Monica had always taken pride in her work, but must concede that there really was no glory in being a model teacher here. Professionalism wasn't valued by either the students or the administration. The teachers who did the least and spoon-fed their students, were the most popular at the university. Students rewarded these teachers for their indulgence, by awarding them the highest ratings on student evaluations. As such, Monica was in a no-win situation, and the joy of teaching that she once felt had vanished. She now dreaded Saturday evenings because work followed on Sunday mornings. Preparing lessons was no longer enjoyable, since the students were by and large unmotivated and unappreciative of her efforts. *Why should I invest all this time and energy in trying to make a class interesting when students don't care?* Monica often wondered. Her students' only concern was getting information that would serve them on their tests. If particular details weren't going to be tested, they couldn't care less about the subject matter. "Teacher, teacher, no need, no need!" was their common refrain when Monica taught lessons that they deemed unnecessary.

The business of tickling her students' butts to apply themselves to their lessons was also getting old. Why should she have to beg them to open their textbooks and coax them to do the assigned exercises? Whether they were productive in class or not, at the end of the month, she still got her paycheck. Moreover, their sense of entitlement to unearned As and their constant whining was <u>really</u> beginning to annoy her. She couldn't get over her pupils' chutzpah in feeling that their gracing her with their presence - although they didn't actively participate in class - was grounds for an automatic

A. Oh, how Monica wished that her pampered chair warmers could realize they are privileged to have access to education that many poor children across the world only dreamt of obtaining someday.

Since she didn't believe in coddling her pupils, all this customer service catering rhetoric that was being promoted by management didn't help matters. While she agreed that teachers needed students to earn their living, and without students, teachers would have no jobs, Monica knew that this kowtowing was doing them a disservice. In the long run, the doling out of all this customer care was going to backfire. And the Kingdom's lofty goal of having an educated and effective Saudi workforce by the year 2030 was destined to remain just that - a vision.

Additionally, Monica found the Saudi policy of no social interaction between unrelated males and females rather irksome. By nature, she preferred the company of males to females. That was because in general, she found men to be more fun, less catty, and judgmental than women. So, at her age, being deprived of the ability to engage in platonic relationships with her male colleagues was rather annoying. Perhaps if Monica was a Saudi woman, she would not mind the gender segregation. However, being a Westerner, this passé system of gender apartheid just struck her as being rather unnatural and unhealthy.

The biggest sign however, that it was time for Monica to seek greener pastures was the presence of ISIS in the community. You can well imagine her shock and dismay when it was reported that two Saudi women had been caught by the campus security officers distributing pamphlets to students. Their brazen recruitment strategy in an environment that should be a safe haven was quite disturbing to her. It was one thing for ISIS to be operating in the boonies, but their presence in Al-Khobar, at Monica's place of employment at that, was a little too close for her comfort. So, she was now actively monitoring the US Embassy's Travel Advisory website. She seriously hoped that it wouldn't become necessary for her to prematurely end her contract. However, if the situation became dire, whether the contract had ended or not, Monica was prepared to jump ship.

CHAPTER

39

YASMIN WAS ABOUT TO SHUT down her computer when a message from the dean popped up on her screen. She groaned after reading it: Urgent! Staff meeting in fifteen minutes, my office. *Oh, come on! Do we really need to have a staff meeting now? Couldn't whatever the dean had to say wait until Sunday morning?*

When Yasmin arrived at the dean's office, a quick scan of her peers seated around the table alerted her to the fact that this staff meeting didn't involve the entire staff. Immediately, she became suspicious that this was no ordinary meeting. She suspected that the dean had something up her sleeve. As was her norm, Dean Martha began her talk by telling her staff members about the college's mission statement and marketing plan to increase student enrollment. While she waxed on about the college's goals, Yasmin began to mentally plan her grocery shopping list for the weekend. Midway through her boss' spiel, Yasmin's head jerked up and her jaw dropped. Did she hear the dean correctly? She couldn't have heard her say what she thought she heard her say. Her eyes darted around the room searching for confirmation in her colleagues' body language. Similar to Yasmin's, their facial expressions also registered shock. With her vintage plastic smile in place, Dean Martha briskly stated, "As you all know, our staff numbers are greatly affected by student enrollment numbers. Both must be in alignment with each other. Since enrollment has dropped significantly this trimester, we are forced to reduce staff numbers. I'm afraid that you'll have to leave this weekend." And with that, she proceeded to distribute to each teacher, their exit visa document.

As soon as the staff members had time to process the dean's words, the room erupted in anger and she was bombarded with comments and questions. "WHAT?! We're terminated?!" "This isn't right." "What about the 25 percent bonus we were promised?" Dean Martha with her customary glibness deflected their angry outbursts. She stood up, and signaled that the meeting had ended by saying, "It's nothing personal ladies, it's just business. You'll receive your flight details shortly via email. Your final salary payment will be electronically deposited into your bank account next month."

The color drained from Yasmin's face. Slowly, she pushed her chair away from the table, and rose weakly to her feet. She grabbed the sides of the table for support. When she felt strong enough to walk back to her office, she walked away with heavy steps. It took all of her strength to clear out her workstation. "This is bollocks - unadulterated bollocks," she repeated over and over as she angrily stuffed her personal belongings into her bag. "It's nothing personal. Yeah, right. Who does she think she's fooling? The old witch surely had her reasons for getting rid of us ten and not the others," she fumed as she exited the college for the last time. Yasmin wouldn't be surprised if this was retribution for having been caught leaving Vicki's place.

Back in her flat, Yasmin hastily started packing her luggage. Her groceries and kitchen appliances, she freely gave away to the Indian workers on the compound. When Yasmin was finished sorting her stuff, she rang her family. "Mum, I'm coming home on Saturday. Can you or Dad please pick me up at the airport? The flight is scheduled to land at nine o'clock in the night." Yasmin's mother sensed that all wasn't well with her daughter. "Yas, you alright? What's going on?" she asked. Yasmin tried to mask the bitterness in her voice, "It's a long story, Mum. We'll talk when I get home."

Yasmin imagined what her life would be like when she returned to Hall Green. After enjoying all this independence, it was going to be hard returning to live with her father and mother. While Yasmin adored her parents, they were a bit old-fashioned. So, it was going to be challenging for her to reside both in their world (which is the world of the ancestors) and the modern British one. She wasn't looking forward to rushing home from a nighttime social event and having to answer to her father about her whereabouts; or being restricted in her interactions with men. Let's face it, she was an adult and quite capable of making her own life choices.

Physically and emotionally drained, Yasmin eased herself down unto the floor and leaned back against her bedroom wall for support. She closed her eyes and tried to make sense of all that had occurred during the last twenty-four hours. Valiantly, Yasmin tried to suppress the anger and resentment that was festering in her heart. After all that she had invested in this bloody start-up: enthusiasm, energy, time, ideas, and labor - she knew that she had been royally screwed. She calmed down a tad when she reflected on the fact that she had at least got to see the holy cities of Makkah and Madinah. Memories of these spiritual journeys boosted her spirits. *So, I got shafted... sometimes, that's how it goes,* Yasmin reminded herself matter-of-factly. While she had lost the physical battle, she would be victorious in the spiritual and emotional fights. She would be damned if she allowed these bastards to grind her down. In the end, they would all have to account to Allah for their actions.

The adhan sounded in the distance. Regaining her composure, Yasmin jumped to her feet. She went into her bathroom to perform wudu in preparation for Salat Maghrib (evening prayers).

After completing her ablutions, she knelt on her prayer mat and read several verses from the Qur'an. Doing so had a very calming effect on her. When she was in the right frame of mind, Yasmin began her commune with Allah. She begged him to be merciful unto her and her peers who were unjustly terminated; and she asked for guidance. When she had finished praying, Yasmin felt as if a huge weight had been lifted from her shoulders. All the tension that she usually had at the nape of her neck and across her shoulders had

vanished. The bitterness that she had been nursing was all gone. Yasmin knew that she was going to be alright. Rising slowly to her feet, she folded her prayer mat and closed the Qur'an.

Refreshed from a solid night's rest, Yasmin got up early the next morning. This was the best that she had felt in quite some time. Completely relaxed, she tackled the few remaining chores in preparation for her departure. When everything had been sorted, she circled her flat and snapped a few photos of the space that she had called home for almost one year. Next, she had marmalade with toast for brunch, and afterwards, checked her email.

Her doorbell rang promptly at one o'clock in the afternoon. It was the driver who was taking her to the airport. Yasmin doubted that she would have the opportunity to return to Al-Khobar. So, on the ride to the airport, her eyes greedily took in the sights one final time. As she looked at the beautiful buildings, thoughts about the hapless laborers from the Indian subcontinent whose sweat, and blood, had made Al-Khobar the desirable city that it now was, flashed across her mind. Silently, she said a little prayer for them.

The airport terminal was crowded. Yasmin spied some of her former colleagues, but had no desire to interact with them. Feelings were clearly mutual; her eyes had locked with theirs and they registered no sign of recognition. *Yep, it was over.*

Her luggage was a couple kilos over the weight allowance, but the kind agent didn't charge her the fee for excess baggage. After clearing the security checkpoint, Yasmin sat in the waiting area at the departure gate for her flight. She had some units left on her cellphone and quickly sent a text message. Satisfied that all the bits and bobs had been taken care of, she took out her Qur'an and read a few verses. One hour later, the boarding announcement was made for her flight. Eagerly, she boarded the plane; silently rejoicing that this bittersweet chapter of her life was over.

CHAPTER

40

MONICA WAS ABOUT TO TAKE a break from grading her students' research papers when her mobile phone beeped with an incoming text message. She picked up her phone and was surprised to see Yasmin's name on the screen. Yasmin had silently exited her life following their brunch in Bahrain. Back in Al-Khobar, Monica would look for Yasmin at Tamimi's, and the Rashid Mall, but she never saw her again. It was as if her new friend had just vanished in thin air.

One of the downsides of teaching EFL was the whimsical nature of relationships. People were here today and gone tomorrow. From an emotional stance, it didn't make sense getting too attached to one's peers. So, while Monica delighted in meeting new people, she no longer fully invested herself in these new relationships. She enjoyed them for as long as they lasted, but when they ended, she moved on. Actually, Monica had a "three strikes you are out policy," with people she was involved with on a personal level. She would extend herself three times to a person before making the decision to let them go. So, after leaving messages on Yasmin's phone three times and getting no response, Monica left her alone. Although she was disappointed by the way things had ended, Monica could understand Yasmin's behavior. She knew enough about the Pakistani culture to not take Yasmin's actions personally.

Abdul himself was keeping a low profile on the compound. After that fateful meeting at the Nomads' Nest, he had stopped hanging out with his western buddies on the compound. While tongues

146

continued to wag about this or that person's indiscretions, there was no talk whatsoever about Abdul. Monica hoped that his dalliances were a thing of the past and he was now truly on the straight and narrow. The few occasions that Abdul's and Monica's paths crossed, he had averted his eyes – clearly trying to avoid her. Not wanting to embarrass him further, Monica, in turn, saw and did not see him.

A staunch believer in closure, she read Yasmin's message.

Monica, I know that you're thinking poorly of me and completely understand. I just wanted to say that I'm sorry and hope that someday, you'll be able to forgive me. I got sacked on Thursday and am now homeward bound. It was a pleasure knowing you. All the best.

Monica smiled and said softly, "No hard feelings. All's forgiven. Safe travels matey." She walked back to her sofa and eyeballed the stack of students' papers remaining on her coffee table. She still had at least another two hours of marking to do. Sighing loudly, she flopped down on the sofa and turned her attention to marking the paper at the top of the pile.

She was relieved that the light at the end of the tunnel was shining quite brightly. Financially speaking, the Kingdom had been good to her. She had been able to save half of her salary; and did quite a bit of travelling in the region. However, Monica had had enough of the BS, the games, and the drama. She was ready to return to New York. There were exactly five working days left between her and her freedom. "Let the countdown begin!" she exclaimed, as she immersed herself in marking the remaining students' papers.

Several of Monica's students rolled their eyes, and one of them rudely turned her back to her when she passed by them in the corridor. Monica smirked and inwardly rejoiced that she would soon be rid of them. *You princesses are going to be in a world of hurt when the oil runs out!* She thought gleefully to herself. Today was the last day of classes. So, Monica had prepared some review materials for her students and would also give them the option to self-study. She was counting on it being a nice and easy day for her because she had already finished marking their term project papers. What a joke! Half of her students neglected to put their names and student ID numbers on their research papers. Since many of them didn't take their assignment seriously, Monica had no qualms about awarding them "joke" marks.

Now that all continuous assessments had been completed, Monica was on easy street. All that was left for her to mark were the final exams. She was not surprised by the results. Only a handful of her students were passing the course. Naturally, the students who had been doing well throughout the term were the ones who were in good academic shape for the final exam. The final exam was worth forty percent of the students' total course grade. Logic would then dictate that students who had a grade below forty-two percent going into the final examination can't pass the course; however, we're talking about Saudi Arabia here, where logic doesn't prevail. So, students who've never passed a quiz, or test all semester, can still pass the course with flying colors because of Wasta. Whatever.

Education is a big business in the Kingdom – and, a complete farce, some cynics might add. The bottom line is the filthy lucre – not student learning. As Monica's immediate superior succinctly put it in their last staff meeting, "We're in the business of passing students, not failing them." So, educators who take their work seriously, will find teaching here a very frustrating experience. This was the reason why the retention rate of teachers in Saudi Arabia was so low. Many arrived with the idea that they were going to subvert the system and improve the culture. When these overzealous teachers eventually realized that they were fighting a losing battle, they become disillusioned, jaded, and eventually resigned.

Others who managed to "hang in there" usually left wondering if all their self-sacrificing was worth it. While Monica didn't regret this teaching experience, if she had it to do again, she would pass on the opportunity. Twelve months could feel like an eternity when the going got tough. In the span of her lifetime, Monica knew that one year was really a small price to pay for all that she had gained along the way. Yes, there was a lot of stress and unnecessary crap to contend with, but that was par for the course. This adventure had taught her a lot about human nature, and more importantly, about herself. Also, it had made her realize how fortunate she was to be born and raised female in the Western hemisphere.

The bell rang, signaling the end of the class and likewise, the semester. "Good luck on your final exams, ladies," Monica chirped as her students rushed out the door. Quickly, she erased the board and gathered her belongings. The bus would be arriving in twenty minutes. She was truly grateful that their workdays had been shortened by three hours during the final two weeks of the term. It was nice having some downtime after the frenetic work pace throughout the year.

There were still a lot of personal things Monica needed to attend to before she departed the Kingdom. For instance, after work, she planned to buy another suitcase and a few practical gifts for her friends. Since Monica doubted that she would pass this way again, she was buying as many locally made products as her budget would allow. Her female friends would receive small bottles of traditional Misk essence. Monica thought that fragrance was absolutely divine! She just loved the fresh, powdery scent of Misk. At nighttime, she liked to dab a little on her pillowcase. The fragrance enhanced her sleep.

Her male buddies who smoke would receive a medium-sized shisha pipe; the nonsmokers would be gifted with bottles of Oud Arabian cologne. Once Monica had picked up those items, she would be good to go. All that would be left for her to do is purchase a few bars of gold for investment purposes, several boxes of dates, and as a special treat for herself, a colorful abaya.

CHAPTER

41

MONICA HAD JUST SPENT THE last three hours cleaning her apartment in preparation for Lauren and Fred's arrival. The three friends were going to celebrate the end of their contract with a farewell dinner at her flat. Chances were slim that their paths would cross again; therefore, Monica wanted everything to be perfect for their get-together.

Yesterday, she went to Tamimi's for the last time. Since Lauren and Fred like spicy food, Monica was going to make Dhaba style dhal and basmati rice. It was a very easy and tasty dish to prepare; Yasmin had given her the recipe. As she picked up the ingredients, naturally, Yasmin came to Monica's mind and she wondered how her pal was doing. She stopped by the Hot Food section and purchased some naan bread to complete the meal. In honor of the occasion, Monica also splurged on two bouquets of freshly cut flowers - one for the centerpiece of the dining table, and the other, for the coffee table in the living room.

The shabby dining table looked fantastic, now that it had been covered with a gorgeous, white embroidered cotton tablecloth that Monica had purchased on sale at Zara Home on a weekend trip to Jeddah. After setting the table with the dinner plates and glassware, she stepped back and admired her handiwork. Satisfied that all was ready for the arrival of her guests, she took a quick shower, and got dressed.

The doorbell rang promptly at seven. Quickly, Monica tossed the green salad, and poured the mango lassi into a chilled glass pitcher. After lighting the four long candlesticks on the dining table, Monica opened her front door. "Welcome! Welcome folks," she greeted Lauren and Fred heartily as they entered her apartment. The friends exchanged a group hug as they knew they may never see each other again. Lauren looked fabulous in a LBD and had piled her hair high on her head in a sophisticated bun. Fred also looked great in a long-sleeved white shirt and a novelty tie. They had thoughtfully brought two bottles of Martinelli's Sparkling Cider with them. Monica filled each of their glasses with the libation and raised hers in the air. "Yay, we made it!" she shouted. Lauren and Fred raised their glasses in unison and the three of them clinked glasses and toasted their survival.

"Gosh, it's finally over," said Lauren somewhat forlornly.

"Hallelujah!" Monica replied. "I'm so relieved to be escaping this fishbowl. This was the longest week of my life. I thought that it would never end!"

The mates burst out laughing. Fred was the perfect gentleman and refilled all their glasses. Lauren raised hers in the air and said, "Here's to a better future." Fred and Monica also raised their glasses and echoed Lauren's sentiment, "To the future!" After they finished their drinks, the friends put their glasses on the coffee table and made their way over to the dining table.

Fred squealed with delight when Monica put the food on the table. "OMG, you made dahl," he said appreciatively. "It is one of my favorite dishes." In between compliments over the meal, the trio talked about their post contract plans. Monica was ecstatic when Lauren and Fred disclosed that they were going to teach in Thailand. "I don't blame y'all," Monica said. "After this hellish contract, you need a chill job and place to live," she continued. They're such a lovely couple; Monica secretly hoped that their relationship would someday lead to marriage. "So, what will you do when you get back to New York?" Lauren asked. "Well, for the first month, I plan to do squat," replied Monica and chuckled. "I just need to decompress. Afterwards, it will be time to spruce up my CV and rejoin the rat race."

The night air was pleasant; so, the friends took their dessert out on the balcony. Fred and Lauren cuddled while they ate in silence. Monica looked out across Al-Khobar; it looked very pretty, ablaze in residential and commercial lights. Animated voices chattered below, and drew her attention back to the compound. Looking down, she saw the usual cliques, clustered in their standard places. *Oh, the interesting stories I'll tell about them someday,* Monica promised herself. As she reflected on all that had transpired during the contract, she observed the trapped fishes in the expat bowl one final time. Then she threw her head back and hooted with laughter.

The End

GLOSSARY

abaya: a traditional black cloak worn by females

adhan: a call to prayer for Muslims made five times a day

alhamdulillah: praise to God

agal: a black cord, worn doubled, used to keep a ghoutrah in place on the Arab man's head

banats: girls

beta: a Pakistani term of endearment for a child

bollocks: a British expression of annoyance

chacha-zaad bhai: an Urdu word that means cousin

cheeky bugger: a British expression for a slightly naughty or mischievous person

dua: an act of supplication

ghoutrah: the head-cloth worn by Saudi men

habibte: an Arabic term of endearment

inshallah: "if Allah or God wills it"

ka'bah: a small, cubical building in the courtyard of the Great Mosque at Mecca containing a sacred black stone

khobz: Middle Eastern flatbread

kurta: a loose, collarless shirt worn by people from South Asia

lengha choli: a traditional bridal outfit originating in the Indian subcontinent

ma'ashallah: Arabic expression for appreciation or joy

nawadir: Arabic story-telling, anecdotes both fictional and non-fictional

nicked: a British expression that means to steal

niqab: veil to cover the face

scrummy: a British expression for delicious

sixes and sevens: a British expression for a state of total confusion, disorder or disarray

thobe: an ankle-length, long-sleeved robe worn by Arab men

whinging: a British expression for fretful complaining

ABOUT THE AUTHOR

FERN HAS BEEN TEACHING EFL since 2005. During this period, she taught in Saudi Arabia for two years. She has an advanced degree in Education Administration and a B.A. in English Literature. This is her first novel.

Printed in the United States
By Bookmasters